I'll go alone if I must.

While I live, Erdas
has a protector.

TALES OF THE
GREAT BEASTS

TALES OF THE
GREAT BEASTS

BRANDON MULL

Nick Eliopulos ◆ Billy Merrell

Gavin Brown ◆ Emily Seife

❖

SCHOLASTIC INC.

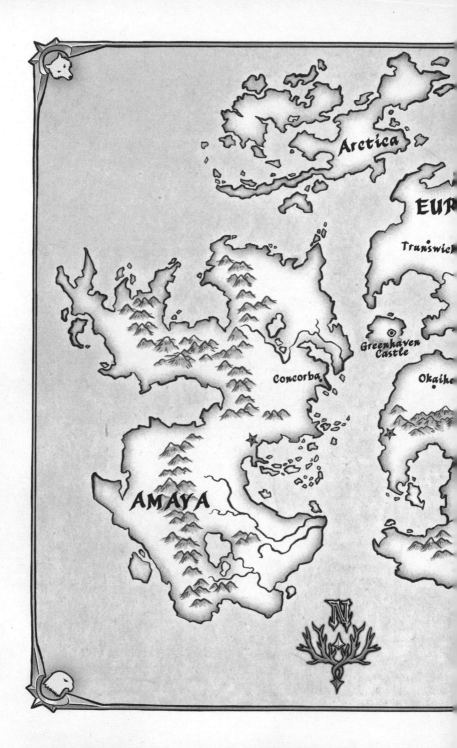

❖

Library of Congress Control Number: 2014940800

ISBN 978-0-545-78709-3
12 11 10 9 8 7 6 5 4 3 2 1   14 15 16 17 18

Book design by Charice Silverman
Map illustration by Michael Walton

Library edition, November 2014

Printed in the U.S.A.   23

Scholastic US: 557 Broadway • New York, NY 10012
Scholastic Canada: 604 King Street West • Toronto, ON M5V 1E1
Scholastic New Zealand Limited: Private Bag 94407 • Greenmount, Manukau 2141
Scholastic UK Ltd.: Euston House • 24 Eversholt Street • London NW1 1DB

Kovo

RISE OF THE REPTILE KING

By Nick Eliopulos

Feliandor, boy king of Stetriol, peered into the shadows, pondering his next move. The ocean was at his back. Before him, a dark forest, and his destiny.

He dug the toe of his boot into the sand and thought of his troubled kingdom. From a hidden pocket in his travel cloak, he pulled out a small glass vial, empty except for a meager drop of amber liquid. He turned the vial in his fingers and watched the droplet catch the fading sunlight.

This liquid held the power to change . . . everything.

It was called the Bile.

Feliandor's father had been a good king, and Feliandor wanted to be a good king too. It was for that reason and that reason alone that he held court. Once a week, the doors to the throne room were opened to any citizen who desired an audience with the king. It was a tradition his father had started years before, and one that had made him immensely popular. "We live in a great tower," he'd once told his son, "but the distance between a king and his subjects should never be greater than a single voice can travel."

And so each week, Feliandor interacted with the people of his kingdom. Usually that meant his subjects would come from far and wide to complain about petty matters while Feliandor listened carefully, nodded thoughtfully, and then offered reassuring words – and, when possible, solutions.

It did not come naturally to him, and it never seemed to get any easier. But he always had two allies beside him through the ordeal: to his left, Salen, the royal adviser, and to his right, Jorick, captain of the king's guard. With the knowledge and power they represented, he felt that he could accomplish nearly anything.

The people seemed determined to put this to the test.

"My king, you must do something," said the man before him now, an aging blacksmith named Gerard. He gestured to the younger man at his side. "He's ruined my livelihood."

The younger man, Donnat, also a blacksmith, crossed his arms defiantly. "The old man hardly needs any help there. It's not my fault he can't keep up with the times! The customers have spoken, and my revolutionary smithing technique –"

"Your smithing technique is pathetic!" Gerard interrupted. "You sacrifice quality for speed. Your swords would shatter against a turtle shell."

"Now he's resorting to slander, Your Majesty. Unless he means to suggest he's actually attacked turtles with my wares."

Feliandor wished he could laugh at the spectacle of two grown men acting in this way, but the hall was crowded with onlookers. If he could solve this problem, it would be proof of his wisdom and prudence – and there was no better time to appear wise than when one had witnesses.

Fel cleared his throat, and the sound echoed. The throne room was ancient and drab, a box of rough stone with narrow slits overhead to let in daylight. The walls had been adorned with colorful tapestries and the ceremonial swords and shields of kings past, but the decorations did little to brighten the gloomy space. It had always felt like a tomb to Fel. Even in happier days.

The throne itself, however, was a masterpiece. Placed upon a stone platform and crafted entirely of Stetriolan iron, the chair was embellished with the features of a half-dozen animals: the outspread wings of a great bird of prey, the patterned scales of a reptile, the clawed feet of some vicious predator. It wasn't comfortable, but it was beautiful. And intimidating. Fel had never seen anything else quite like it, and he doubted either of the smiths before him were capable of such craft.

He turned his gaze on the older of the two, Gerard. "But *he* was *your* apprentice?" he asked.

"That's right," the older smith huffed. "And I thought that once I gave up on teaching him, this louse would set up shop elsewhere. Not two doors down from my anvil, which has been serving our town for generations!"

Donnat shrugged. "Every town in Stetriol has an established blacksmith. How am I supposed to earn a living if the older generation won't get out of the way?"

"I see," Fel said. "So there's not enough smithing work to go around. Does that about sum it up?"

"That's right," Gerard said. "I'm not afraid of a little competition, but I won't resort to this charlatan's tactics."

"Then you'll never beat my prices," Donnat said lightly.

Feliandor turned to his adviser and lowered his voice. "Salen, what do you have for me?"

"Hm, yes," Salen said slowly, stroking his white beard . . . slowly. Salen did everything slowly. "This raises some interesting questions . . . concerning the crown's role in commerce. I'd like to set up a committee led by key figures from the merchants' guild, and open discussions—"

Feliandor rolled his eyes dramatically. "Salen, so help me, if you put me in one more meeting, I'll have you exiled. I want a solution right now." He turned to his other side. "Any ideas, Jorick?"

Jorick grunted in a way that perfectly communicated his lack of patience for squabbling merchants. "I could take each of them in hand and smash them together until we had a single large blacksmith where before there were two scrawny blacksmiths."

Fel smiled despite himself. "Excellent thought, Jorick, but let's call that Plan B." He cleared his throat again, silencing the mutterings of the crowd, and returned his attention to the men who awaited his judgment. "All right, all right. If the problem, at heart, is that there is not enough smithing work, then let me see about throwing some business your way. It's about time the king's guard was outfitted with new equipment. It's a big enough job to keep you both tending your fires for months. Is this acceptable?"

The older smith nodded. "It would be my honor to provide arms and armor to the guard."

The younger smith smiled. "But I could do it twice as fast for a fraction of the cost."

"None of that," Feliandor admonished. "There will be no shortcuts, and you'll each receive the same rate for your work. See my quartermaster on the way out, and he'll get you started."

Fel turned a smug smile on his adviser as the two men left the hall. "There, see? Everyone leaves happy."

Salen didn't return the king's smile. "A short-term solution, my king, merits only a short celebration."

"Why, thank you, Salen, I believe a celebration would be lovely. I'll ask you to make the arrangements. Now, what's next?" He turned to the page whose job it was to keep the proceedings orderly. He rubbed his hands together in anticipation. "Who has another knot for their king to untangle?"

The page paled. "Apologies, King Feliandor, but that is all for today."

"Surely not!" Fel scoffed and looked about the room. There were several dozen people in attendance. Had they all come simply to gawk? Fel thought they should be falling over themselves for the opportunity to speak directly to their king.

As his eyes roamed the hall, they fell upon a woman he'd never seen before. Though she was but one face among the crowd, she stood out immediately as Niloan. It was more than her dark skin that marked her as such. Equally striking were the Niloan garments she wore — finery of vibrant primary colors, the kind one could only achieve with Niloan dyes produced by Niloan craftsmen using Niloan plants. Garments so colorful were a luxury in Stetriol, and rare.

A foreigner at his court was an unusual enough thing that Feliandor took instant notice, and he wondered what business she had there. Her bearing was regal, her chin held high. Was it possible that she was there as a representative of Niloan royalty? And if so, why hadn't she presented herself, as was the custom?

Suddenly Feliandor felt very much on display.

"I know," he said loudly. "Let's have an update on the arbor project. Where is Xana?"

There was a rustling in the crowd as a Stetriolan woman stepped forth. Xana never wore the traditional skirts of a woman of the court, favoring instead the more practical trousers and boots as befit her role as the region's foremost botanist. Even her finest tunic, which she wore now, showed the mark of her profession, lightly stained by grass and dirt.

She bowed before the king, then rose and looked him in the eye. "Forgive me, my king, but I haven't prepared an update."

"No need to be so formal, Xana." Feliandor smiled. "I am simply curious to know of any progress."

"There is no progress to report, I'm afraid."

Salen lifted a gnarled finger. "My king, perhaps it would be best to allow Xana the opportunity to prepare an official report. I'd be happy to schedule a time—"

Feliandor moaned loudly. "I'm sure you would, Salen. I'm sure nothing would make you happier." He rose from the throne, taking a step down toward Xana, who stood at attention at the foot of the platform's steps. "I'd simply like to know what your people have been up to this past month. Have you planted any trees?"

Xana nodded. "We planted four hundred saplings imported from foreign lands. Twelve different species. Of those, only thirty percent survived."

"Thirty percent! Well, that's . . ." Feliandor paused. "That's more than one hundred trees that weren't there before. That's something."

Xana shook her head, less nervous now that she was in her element. "None of the trees will last a year. Their root structures are meant for hardier topsoil. Those plants that don't die from lack of nutrients and water will eventually grow too big for their own roots. They'll simply topple over."

Fel bristled. He felt the eyes of the crowd on him, but kept his gaze locked on Xana. "Very well," he said, hoping he sounded calm and full of grace. "I will double your budget for the next quarter, Xana, but you must promise me that you'll have something to show for it."

"I cannot do that, my king."

"Can't promise me results?"

"I mean that I cannot in good conscience accept any more of the crown's gold. To change the flatlands into a forest requires not just trees, but an entirely different environment. Short of learning to control the weather, I don't know what else we can do."

Fel stood silent, feeling his anger and disappointment like a physical force. His face radiated heat, and he knew that he was blushing before the entire crowd. He clenched his fists and ground his teeth together, but the more he fought the sensation, the warmer his cheeks grew.

He caught sight of the Niloan woman again, who watched him without a hint of emotion. When their eyes met, he was the first to look away.

Xana appeared nervous again as the silence dragged on. Finally she spoke up. "I'm so sorry, my king. The climate is too arid. The soil is all but infertile. There will be no forest at the heart of Stetriol."

Suddenly the heavy doors to the room were thrown open, and a loud bang echoed throughout the space. All heads turned to the entrance, where a mangy, wild-eyed man with a scraggly beard hobbled into view, carrying a soiled canvas sack.

Jorick drew his sword. His men, stationed throughout the room, did the same.

"Hold," said the king, placing a steadying hand on Jorick's sword arm.

"Good King Fel!" the man cried out in a singsong voice. "Good King Fel, the Good King Fel, now all that's left is you." It sounded like a line from a song, but Feliandor couldn't place the tune.

"State your business," Jorick barked.

The man continued his slow shuffle toward the throne, and the crowd parted to let him pass. He hoisted the sack higher onto his shoulder, grunting before he answered.

10

"I've been to the other side, and now I'm back. He told me to. Like I told Jace not to die. But nobody listens!"

Salen gave a start of surprise, then took a step toward Feliandor. "That is Lord Griswald," he hissed in the king's ear.

Fel's jaw dropped. "By the Beasts, you're right. I was sure the man was dead."

Lord Gareth Griswald was a national hero, most famous for being the first person to reach the peak of Mount Crimson, tallest of the Red Mountains. It was that accomplishment that had made him the natural choice for Feliandor's very first pronouncement as king: Griswald would lead a team of explorers beyond the Red Mountains, into the heart of Stetriol, and out the other side.

While the coastline of the island nation was well documented and heavily settled, few had ventured into the interior of the continent. Everything they'd seen had led them to believe the entire interior was an arid wasteland. Yet Feliandor had always held out hope that somewhere beyond view was an oasis. Perhaps a great interior lake surrounded by lush forests, or an overgrown caldera suitable as farmland.

But Griswald had disappeared beyond the mountains more than a year ago. And he did not have the look of a man who had spent the time enjoying an oasis.

Feliandor raised his arms and raised his voice. "People of Stetriol! Lord Griswald is returned."

If his intention had been to calm the crowd, he had failed. A murmur passed through it, a thread of shock and horror as the people realized the man before them was their lost hero, returned to them in much worse shape than he'd left.

He was close enough now that Feliandor could smell the sour stink of him, like milk left out in the sun.

"Uh, my good man," Fel said so that everyone could hear, "you've clearly been through an ordeal. Let's set you up with a bath and a hot meal. Salen here can schedule a time for us to talk."

It might have been Fel's imagination, but Griswald's sack seemed to be . . . moving.

"Jace died," the man said.

Fel turned to Salen. "Jace?" he whispered.

"One of his party," the adviser answered under his breath. "The young cartographer."

"I wrote it down to remember," Griswald said from the center of the hall, shuffling still closer. "Jace died by toad, Janas by bee. Marcus . . . Marcus by thirst 'neath a lone pine tree."

"Oh, my . . . His entire party is dead," Salen said.

"Get him out of here, Jorick," Fel hissed.

Jorick signaled to his men and took a step forward. Despite Griswald's obvious delirium, the advancing guards were not lost on him.

"No!" the man shouted. He gripped the sack and swung it off of his shoulder, wielding it like a weapon. "No, I must give the king his gift!"

Salen put a hand on Fel's shoulder. "My king . . ."

Fel's feet felt rooted in place.

As the guards approached Griswald from all sides, the man turned over the sack, dumping its contents on the throne room floor.

Snakes. Dozens of them. They writhed upon the ground like a sinister kaleidoscope, all color and slither and hiss.

And then they began to untangle themselves and launch off in every direction.

The hall exploded into chaos. As the guards descended upon the snakes with their swords, bystanders fled for the doors, shoving and shouting. Griswald stood in the center of the room, cackling. A scream rang out, and Fel saw a particularly speedy snake launch itself at a little girl, baring its fangs. Before the snake could strike, a streak of brown appeared, slicing it in two. The streak was an animal, moving so quickly across the stone floor that Fel could not get a good view of it, but it looked like a rodent of some kind, long and sinuous, almost snakelike itself.

"You rule a kingdom of dust and snakes!" Griswald howled. "There is nothing beyond the mountains but death!"

And then Jorick was dragging Fel backward, to the doorway hidden in the curtains behind the throne. The captain shoved him inside before turning back to the chaos of the throne room. Salen followed Fel through the doorway and barred the door behind them.

In the sudden dark, with the screams of his subjects still echoing beyond the door, Fel felt overwhelmed and much younger than his years. For a moment, he was a boy again, and Salen was the grandfatherly figure he'd known his entire life. Fel teetered into the old man's arms, trembling. If Salen was surprised, he didn't show it, only held Fel until he had composed himself once more.

"Are you all right, Fel — my king?" Salen asked, his hand upon Fel's shoulder.

"I want that man in the dungeons," Fel said, straightening his iron crown.

"But he's a hero. The people—"

"Just do it, Salen. Lock him up and throw away the key."

That night, Feliandor was restless. Little wonder, after the day he'd had.

He found himself wandering the halls of the castle, which were never truly dark nor fully empty. Candles remained lit throughout the night for the benefit of the guards stationed around the castle. The soldiers stood rigid and expressionless, so much so that Fel often failed to even think of them as people. They were more like the castle's furniture.

At length he came to the great hall, where the portraits of Stetriol's kings were on display. He walked past the procession of his ancestors, coming to a stop just below the painting of his parents. They had bucked tradition by insisting that both king and queen appear together in the official state portrait. They had always acted as equals.

And if Feliandor's father had been loved by the people, well, his mother had practically been worshipped. She had walked among their subjects at every opportunity, championing public health projects and—to the nobility's dismay—public literacy. It had been an eccentric cause, but to the surprise of her detractors, the people took to it with great zeal.

Working together, his parents had left Stetriol better than they'd found it. There was no debating that. It was a fact.

It was Feliandor's rotten luck that he had inherited a kingdom at its peak. It had nowhere to go but down. Stetriol was in a state of decline. Many people throughout the land were looking for a scapegoat, someone to blame as their lives became more difficult. They didn't blame geography or weather patterns. They blamed their king.

Fel studied the portrait now. For the hundredth time he looked for something of himself in his parents' faces. It was as if he'd inherited only their plainest features – and their problems.

Stetriol's decline wasn't his fault; Fel, at least, knew this. The coasts were vibrant, rich with life and graced with moderate weather. Just a little bit inland, though, the coastal area ran into the Red Mountains, a range that ringed the interior of the continent. And that interior was arid, inhospitable, home to ghastly, venomous animals and little else.

The vast expanse of Feliandor's kingdom was unable to support human life, and the coasts were getting crowded. Thanks in part to his parents' reforms, the populations of the coastal towns were booming. The people had nowhere to go. There wasn't enough work. Poverty was rampant, and that had led to crime and unrest.

The arbor project had been his last desperate hope. If the land was the problem, then he would change the land. He had sent a dozen of the kingdom's most able colonists to erect a temporary settlement just on the other side of the mountains. Their goal: to manipulate the soil so that it could support a wider variety of plant life. He wanted Stetriol to boast a Niloan jungle or a Euran forest.

But everything they had planted would die.

Movement near the ground caught Fel's attention. At first he feared it was a snake, escaped from the afternoon's grim adventure. But then he saw it clearly. It was a mammal – the same rodent-like creature he'd seen in the throne room earlier that day.

"Hello there," Fel said. "What are you up to?" He realized too late that he must sound childish to the guard standing sentry in the hallway.

The creature stood on its hind legs, clicked its teeth at him, then fell to its four feet and walked away. It stopped partway up the hall and turned its head to look back at him.

"You want me to follow you?" Fel asked.

The mammal clicked again, then continued up the path. Its obvious intelligence left no doubt – this was a spirit animal. Fel had suspected as much when he'd seen it earlier, though he knew it didn't belong to any of his guards. His curiosity was piqued. He turned to the nearby guard. "You there," he said, and the sentry somehow managed to stand even straighter. "Come with me. And stay close."

The animal led them to an outside courtyard. The night air was balmy and smelled of the ocean. For a moment, Fel felt a rush of joy. The best days of his childhood had been spent at the beach, away from the drab castle, and the smell of salt water on the wind was enough to take him back to more carefree times – but only momentarily. Then a figure stepped from the shadows, and the guard at Fel's back drew his sword. Fel remembered very suddenly that his life had not been carefree in some time.

The figure dropped to one knee. "I come in peace," she said.

Fel recognized her instantly as the Niloan woman from the throne room. He held out a hand to stop the guard's advance. "Hold. It's all right." He looked over his shoulder at the guard and lifted an eyebrow. "But keep your sword ready." He turned back to the woman, who remained on one knee and kept her gaze cast upon the ground – although the furry animal now stood atop her shoulder and glared brazenly back at him.

"I don't suppose you're here because Nilo has reconsidered the terms of our latest trade agreement." Until recently, Nilo's need for iron had been a major source of income for Stetriol. That had changed when Nilo's rulers cut a deal with the new Amayan government, who sold their ore for practically nothing.

But the woman was not there to discuss iron. "I'm afraid not, Your Majesty," she said.

"Please stand."

She did as he said, meeting his eyes. She was quite a bit taller than him, and the animal on her shoulder only made her seem bigger. But Fel would not be intimidated in his own home.

"The animal is yours?"

"Vox. My spirit animal." With a flash of light, the animal disappeared, and in its place was a serpentine black tattoo winding around her shoulder and upper arm. "He is a mongoose. They are native to my homeland."

"So you are Niloan. But not here on state business."

"I am here on behalf of another. A benefactor who has asked me to present you with a gift." She spoke flatly, without a hint of emotion, which only served to stoke the fires of Fel's impatience.

"Surely this could wait until daylight. My adviser, Salen, likes nothing more than to fill my schedule."

"I approached your adviser earlier today, my liege. But he turned me away."

"Excuse me?"

"I attempted to go through the proper channels. Your Salen wished to keep us from meeting. Yet I simply could not leave without taking the opportunity to speak with you."

Fel smiled to mask his concern. Something wasn't right here. "Well, then this gift must be good."

"Greater than you could dream." She gestured to a satchel at her hip, eyeing the guard at Fel's shoulder, clearly hesitant to make any sudden moves. "May I?"

"Of course."

She reached into the satchel, producing a slender, stoppered glass vial — the type alchemists used for their elixirs. And indeed there was liquid of some kind within it. She held the vial between her thumb and forefinger. "This is known as the Bile," she said. "The name is a joke of sorts. Despite the taste, I assure you it's quite a wonder."

"Ah, let me guess." Feliandor crossed his arms. "A cure-all tincture. Your mysterious benefactor is a great mixer of medicines and elixirs, and he'd like a royal endorsement. You know, I once tried an elixir for vitality, and it turned my tongue green for a week."

"This is nothing like that, my liege." The woman bared her teeth in an exultant smile. "What would you say if I told you that Vox and I have been acquainted for only three months' time?"

"I'd say you were lying. Spirit animals manifest by the

age of thirteen or not at all. And without meaning any offense, I can tell that you . . . are not thirteen."

"And you *are* thirteen. Does it not strike you as unfair?" She hazarded a small step forward. "That you should have so much power, yet no say in whether you are among the chosen who become Marked?"

Feliandor shrugged. "I'm learning that power brings with it very few perks. And my parents did just fine without spirit animals of their own. *Chosen* may be overstating it."

"Yet you seem like a man who is loath to leave anything to chance. Your arbor project, for example . . ."

"Yes, well, there's a lesson in that debacle somewhere too."

"The lesson, if I may, could be this: If you cannot change your land, then why not change your people?"

Feliandor was silent at that. Eventually she continued.

"With one dose of this liquid, a person of any age can force the spirit animal bond upon any natural animal. And with that bond comes power—the power to become fiercer, faster, and stronger than before. I myself can attest to this. I have benefitted immensely from my association with Vox."

Fel grunted. "It sounds excellent, but believe it or not, one of the first things they tell you as king is not to drink anything a stranger hands you."

"This sample is yours, to do with as you wish." She stooped low and placed the vial on the ground, then stood and took a step back. "I have left a second gift in your throne room: a caged bird. If you find the Bile to your liking and would care to meet my patron, simply release the bird into the wild. That will be the signal that you are ready to meet upon a certain beach in the Hundred Isles – the locals call it Nightshade Island. If the bird is not released within five days, or if you release the bird but fail to arrive shortly thereafter, my benefactor shall move on to others who may be more interested in his offer."

"This is absurd." Fel spoke the words harshly, but his eyes were on the vial. "How did you get into the throne room?"

"The mongoose steps lightly, and now, so do I. Five days, my king. Think on it." In a blur, she ducked back into the shadows and hurdled over the garden wall, faster than Feliandor had ever seen a human move before. She moved, to his mind, more like the mongoose than a person.

And she had left behind not just the vial, but a tattered scroll as well.

When Salen stormed into Feliandor's room at dawn, Jorick at his heel, the king was still dressed, having not slept at all.

"My king!" Salen said, spittle flying into his beard. "What is this the guards tell me of you . . . you entertaining a dangerous stranger in the middle of the night?"

Salen was as angry as he'd ever seen him. But Feliandor was angrier.

"Oh, I assure you, Salen, that she was the one entertaining me. She left this behind." His tone was icy as he unrolled a scroll – the type that his subjects liked to circulate and post in taverns ever since his mother had succeeded in raising the literacy rate.

The centerpiece of the scroll was a crudely drawn cartoon. It bore the legend "Fool's Gold," and featured a caricature of Feliandor—his sharp nose was a dramatic beak, his bushy eyebrows resembled caterpillars, and he practically swam in his oversized clothing: A huge crown fell over his ears and a cape trailed behind him like a curtain. The comically short cartoon king stood upon a footstool, straining to reach a potted plant, which he was watering with a tin jug, the type gardeners used. Only "watering" wasn't the right word, for pouring forth from the jug was not water but coins.

In the background, a family of beggars looked on, starving as their king poured gold onto a plant.

"Is this what people think of me?" Feliandor seethed. "Is this what they say behind my back?"

"Patience, my king," Salen urged, his own anger completely gone. "This is the work of but one person. Do not presume he speaks for all your subjects."

"Is that so? And how many of my subjects have laid eyes on this drawing or another like it? How many will easily forget it? It is incendiary! It is unforgivable. I would have this 'artist' brought before me."

"I would advise—"

"I would advise you keep your opinion to yourself, Salen. This is a matter of security, and therefore falls under Jorick's purview. Not yours." He turned to Jorick, who seemed surprised to be drawn into the argument. "Captain, have the person responsible for this brought in immediately."

Jorick nodded slowly, in the manner of someone who was carefully contemplating what he would say next.

"Am I to understand, my king, that this person is to be arrested?"

Feliandor paused only for a moment. "Yes. And why not? To undermine the king in this way . . . it is dangerous. Have him thrown into the dungeon until I say otherwise."

Salen clucked his tongue and shook his head sadly.

"Enough, Salen. I'm not in the mood." Feliandor threw the scroll down upon the desk as he turned to exit the room. "And I'm not that short!"

Late that night, Fel found himself once again before the portrait of his parents. He tried to imagine their faces distorted by a petty cartoonist's hand. He couldn't picture it, couldn't find the flaws that the artist would need to exploit.

The vial of liquid was in his pocket. His fingers had kept finding it in idle moments throughout the day. Salen and Jorick both knew he had it, but he'd managed to avoid being alone with them since the morning's confrontation. He knew that wouldn't last.

He turned away from his parents to regard the nearest sentry. He was fairly confident it was the same man who had held the post the night before.

Fel took the vial from the pocket and lifted it into view. "You know what this is?" he asked the guard.

"It is called Bile, my king," the man said, standing rigid and unblinking.

Fel smirked. "And does your captain know what it is?"

The guard swallowed, anxiety creeping into his eyes if not his stance. "He does, my king. I told him all I knew of it, my king. He and the royal adviser." He swallowed again. "As is my duty."

"I see," said Fel. He cradled the vial in his palm, looking upon it as he addressed the guard. "How . . . dutiful. Tell me, guardsman, what would you have done if the woman last night had become hostile?"

"I would have fought her, my king."

"And if she had loosed an arrow, aimed for my heart?"

"I would have stopped it, my king."

"Even if the only way to stop it had been to step before it?"

"Even so, my king." The guard had the good sense not to hesitate.

"And if I were to tell you I intended to drink this potentially harmful substance?"

Fel brought his eyes up to the guard, who kept his own eyes forward. He had obviously not been prepared for the shift in the line of questioning.

"I would . . . I would stop you?" he ventured.

"Would you!" Fel said, nearly laughing. "Would you stop me?"

"Of course not, my king," the guard said quickly. "I would never . . ."

Fel couldn't help feeling a pang of pity for the man.

"Here's what I'm truly wondering, guardsman. I'm wondering whether you would drink the substance first. Would that not be a bit like stepping before an arrow? A bit better, in fact." Fel smiled. "I should think you stood a better chance with the liquid."

The guardsman opened his mouth, but his answer was cut off by Jorick's voice, echoing from down the hallway: "Leave the boy alone."

At first Fel thought that the captain had called *him* a boy, but then he realized that Jorick had been referring to the sentry. Was he particularly young for a guardsman? It was true he didn't have the facial hair that was the popular style among Jorick's men.

Fel turned to face Jorick as he approached. "I don't intend to make any of your people drink it," Fel said. He couldn't keep the defensiveness from his voice. "It's only a little logic game."

"I'll drink it," Jorick said.

"You?" Fel said with a sense of genuine surprise – and a flash of guilt.

"Your logic is . . . logical," Jorick explained. "But I cannot ask anything of my men that I wouldn't first do myself."

Fel began to protest, but Jorick placed a large hand upon his shoulder. It was such a fatherly gesture that the king fell instantly silent.

"I know when you've got it in your head to do something. And regardless of what some idiot has scrawled on a scroll, I believe in you."

Fel didn't trust his voice, so he only nodded in gratitude.

"I've never forgiven myself for not being there, you know," Jorick said softly. "When your parents were killed."

"Neither have I," Fel said without thinking, and a part of him regretted it instantly. But the larger part knew that it was true. Jorick should have been there to protect his parents or die trying. That had been his job. It was the most important job in the world, and he'd failed.

The palace menagerie was a marvel. Feliandor had heard of such gardens in other places that were little better than dungeons, with bars that ran from floor to ceiling and concrete floors scattered with hay. Not so here. Great care had been taken to re-create the natural environment of each animal. The downside to this was that the animals could hide from view, spending hours at a time hidden in a tree or behind a rock formation. But as a child, with endless hours of free time stretched before him, Feliandor had known great patience. If he waited long enough and remained still and quiet, the animals always revealed themselves to him.

He had no such luxury now, of course. "Which animal appeals most to you?" he asked Jorick. "If it is not within view, I will have the gamekeeper bring it forth."

Feliandor's eyes roamed over the exhibits, wondering what his own choice would be. There were kangaroos, of course, with their powerful tails, and the spritely sugar glider, a possum with flaps of skin that functioned almost like wings. The thylacine was striped and doglike but with a pouch, and the kookaburra was a large bird with a call that sounded eerily like human laughter. The platypus had always seemed ridiculous to Fel, with its bird parts affixed to a mammal's body, and the koala, while adorable, struck him as a particularly useless choice of spirit animal, dozing all day in its eucalyptus tree.

He sighed. How was it that even the animals of Stetriol were less impressive than those of other lands? Where were their lions, their bears?

As if in answer to his unspoken question, Jorick held out a finger. He pointed to a large, fenced enclosure, beyond which Feliandor could see nothing but shrubbery. Yet he knew what animal lived within.

"You're sure?" he asked.

"I am a warrior at heart, my king," Jorick answered. "There is no better match for me here."

"Very well," Feliandor answered, and he felt his pulse quicken. His eyes scanned the plants on the other side of the fence, seeing nothing, and then all at once falling upon the animal, which had been there all along, hidden among the leaves, watching them with what the young king could have sworn was hate.

The cassowary was among the largest birds in the world, but it looked to Feliandor almost like a reptile. It stood six feet tall on two powerful scaled legs and weighed in at nearly two hundred pounds. Its feathers were black and stiff — not at all attractive — and its bare head and neck rose serpentlike from the mass of dirty feathers, bright blue, with two red wattles hanging low. Growing from the top of its head was a cracked, bonelike projection that looked much like the horn of a rhinoceros and ran right into its long, sharp beak.

But its head, while intimidating, was not its most deadly feature. Feliandor looked down to its three-toed feet, like huge lizard claws, which each featured a daggerlike talon on the inner toe. This claw was lethal. It could kill a man in the blink of an eye.

Feliandor had always been terrified of this beast. It had a tendency to stare at him from behind its fence, and the flat, golden eyes set in that absurd blue face always made him feel as if the bird was challenging him somehow. Daring him to release it. He imagined it holding his eyes with its own while it lifted its claw to his vulnerable belly. . . .

"So be it!" he chirped now, pulling his eyes away from the monstrous bird. "A fine choice."

Feliandor drew the vial from his pocket and considered it for a moment. He felt he should say something, that he should somehow mark the occasion. But words failed him, and in the end he simply handed the vial to Jorick.

Jorick too was silent. He nodded, uncorked the stopper, and held the vial to his lips. His eyes found Feliandor's. In that moment, the young king almost told him to stop, to reconsider. But Feliandor bit back the protest, remaining quiet. Jorick winked once and downed the contents of the vial.

Fel watched the man's face carefully. Jorick winced, as if tasting something bitter, but otherwise seemed unaffected. He turned to regard the cassowary.

"Well?" Feliandor said when he could bear the silence no longer.

"I think I'd like to open the gate," Jorick said.

Feliandor handed him the gamekeeper's key, then took a step back. He looked on as Jorick walked to the gate, unlocked it, and then opened the door. The cassowary still didn't move, and Feliandor watched Jorick watch it.

"Well?" he said again.

And then, suddenly, chaos. The bird rushed forward,

slamming into the half-open door and sending Jorick sprawling back. It hissed, a sound Feliandor had never heard in all his years of coming here. In two great strides the predator closed the gap between itself and the king, and it leaped, clawed talons outstretched. The king stumbled back, bringing up his arms to cover his face and throat, realizing too late that he'd left his stomach exposed. He closed his eyes . . .

And all was silent and still.

Feliandor opened his eyes and let out a short, sudden sob. The bird was gone. Jorick stood by the fence, holding out his arm, and Fel could see the mark on the captain's hand, a tattoo in the shape of a cassowary. Its long neck wrapped up and around his forearm like a snake.

"My king, I'm so sorry. Are you well?"

Feliandor was shaken, but he smiled. "You called it to its dormant state?"

"I've never known it to happen so soon after the partnership is forged."

"That's because the bird is not your partner, Jorick." Feliandor's smile widened. "It is your slave."

Feliandor watched as Jorick went through a series of exercises. Mere hours after drinking the Bile, he was already demonstrating the benefits of his bond with the bird. He was faster, stronger; the grace of his movements was breathtaking. His sparring technique had always been impressive, but now he took on a dozen of his best men without missing a beat.

He already seemed to be favoring a two-handed dagger fighting style over the traditional sword technique, as if in imitation of the bird.

It was extraordinary. And it was the solution to all of Feliandor's problems. If he couldn't improve Stetriol for the people, then he could improve the people of Stetriol. Make them stronger and tougher. Empower them. And they would love him for it. Finally they would love him as they had his father.

A soldier burst into the room and dropped immediately to one knee. "Forgive the interruption, my liege, but I thought you should know . . . Salen intends to harm the bird."

Feliandor laughed a short, surprised bark of a laugh. He turned his eyes on the six-foot, blade-clawed predator in the corner. "What, that bird?"

"No, my king," the soldier said. "The sparrow in the throne room. He has taken it."

Feliandor hurried through the twisting hallways of the castle, Jorick and a dozen other guards at his heels.

"Go on!" he told Jorick. "Run ahead! You're faster than any of us now."

He did, tearing off ahead of them and disappearing into the darkness at the end of the hall, the cassowary at his side. Feliandor experienced a momentary sense of unease as he watched them go. He couldn't say why; he simply preferred to have that bird where he could keep an eye on it.

But his unease gave way to fury as he closed the distance to the throne room. That sparrow was his only link to his new benefactor. His only link to the Bile. Without it, he was back where he'd started, and all his plans amounted to nothing.

Feliandor crossed the threshold and almost couldn't believe the scene before him.

There was Salen, on his knees before Jorick. The captain's face showed such rage, he appeared almost inhuman. He stood menacingly above the old man, who seemed to be in shock and gripped his stomach tightly—as blood spread across his tunic.

The cassowary loomed in the background, Salen's blood upon its claws.

"Salen!" Fel cried. He ran into the room and dropped to his knees before his adviser, placing his hands over the old man's own bloodstained fingers, as if he could forcefully fix the tear in the man's gut. Salen's wide eyes found Fel's, but he said nothing.

"Jorick, what's wrong with you? Guards! Get a healer in here immediately."

Half of the guards who'd accompanied the king into the room turned and left. Jorick seemed to come back to himself, blinking furiously. "My king, I . . . I don't know what came over me. I caught him with the bird. He was going to kill it, and I . . . It felt as if I wasn't in control of my own body. It all happened so quickly."

Fel gently lowered Salen to the ground, one hand behind the old man's head and the other still over his torn stomach, providing pressure to stanch the flow of blood.

"You old fool," Fel hissed. "What possessed you?"

"Trying . . . to protect you." Salen's voice was weak, but his eyes were clear.

"I'm not a child anymore, Salen. I don't need your protection. And you have no right to make decisions that are mine and mine alone."

Even now, Fel could feel the anger coming back, threatening to overtake him. He hated to see Salen hurt, but it was his own fault. This had been a betrayal. It had been treason.

"Listen," Salen whispered. "Listen." And Fel brought his ear down low. "There is a . . . hunger in you," Salen said. "It drives you. It could . . . drive you to greatness." He licked his lips. "But appetite in a king can be a terrible thing."

The healer arrived then, shooing Fel away. He backed off, watching the man work, feeling numb, trying to wipe the blood from his hands. He almost tripped over the birdcage that lay on the floor. The sparrow flitted about inside, unharmed.

"He'll live," the healer said. "But he has an unpleasant few months ahead of him."

"Let's get him to his bedchamber, men," Jorick said.

"No," said Fel. He bent over and opened the little door in the birdcage, and the sparrow flew free, darting immediately out the window and into the night. "Take him to the dungeon," Fel said. "With the rest of the traitors."

Two days later, Feliandor stood upon the beach—not the beach of his native Stetriol, not the beach of his joyful childhood, but a small, misty key in the nearby Hundred Isles. The emissary had called it Nightshade Island.

With the exception of Jorick, he had left his entire entourage behind on the ship. Jorick had rowed the two of them to shore in a small boat, and he stood now, sheltering the king from the wind coming off the water.

"I think you'll find what you're looking for in the forest," Jorick said, indicating the tree line ahead.

"Right," said Feliandor. "Well, come on, then."

"No," said Jorick. Feliandor turned to look at the captain of the guard. There was a flatness to his voice, and an odd quality to his eyes that Feliandor couldn't remember seeing before. His pupils were dilated into wide black discs, and the flinty captain's irises shone oddly yellow in the sun. He had called the cassowary to its active state, and it regarded the king with its equally disconcerting gaze. "You must proceed from here alone."

Somehow it didn't even occur to Feliandor to argue. He merely clutched his travel cloak to his chin and stepped forward, leaving Jorick alone with his monstrous bird.

The forest was quiet, eerily so after the noisiness of the sea, which the flora somehow dampened. Mist swirled about his feet. What exactly was he meant to find here?

The answer became clear soon enough as he stepped into a clearing. Ahead, there was a dramatic rustling of tree and brush, as if the forest were beset by powerful winds. One tree snapped near its base and fell to the side with a crash. Fel pivoted on his toes as if to run, but he couldn't tear his eyes away from the swaying canopy and the darkness beyond—darkness that appeared to be moving, writhing like the snakes in Griswald's sack.

But it wasn't the darkness that was moving. It was fur, black as night. A huge figure emerged from the depths of the forest. Fel had an immediate impression of its size and little else. His brain worked slowly, piecing together the parts his eyes fell upon as they worked their way up, up: the massive gray fist with its knuckles in the dirt, the ropy muscles beneath matted fur, the cavernous nostrils, and the eyes — eyes that were almost human. Almost.

It was an ape, he realized — a gorilla the size of a castle turret.

And in an instant, Feliandor knew that this was the Great Beast of legend. Kovo.

His breath left his lungs. His hands trembled. And then he did something he'd never done before.

He bowed.

He was on his knees for only a moment before a deep, sonorous voice boomed through the trees — or did it only boom through his head?

"Arise, Feliandor," said the beast. "I would see you on your feet. For are we not equals?"

Feliandor rose slowly, bringing his head up last of all, raising his eyes to look Kovo in the face. The Great Beast looked ancient, with deep grooves lining his pitch-black features, but his power was unmistakable . . . and humbling.

"Forgive me," Fel said, "but are we equals? I . . . I never thought to meet —"

"You are among the five most powerful and important humans on the planet," Kovo said. "I am one of fifteen Great Beasts. By my count, that makes you the rarer and more precious of us two."

"I . . . If it pleases you, yes." Feliandor felt like an idiot. He had rested on courtly manners for so long—he had no idea how to act when the rules had fallen away so quickly. And his voice sounded small and weak behind the pounding of his heart.

"It pleases me to please powerful men, my king. And it would please me greatly to ease your burdens."

"My burdens are . . . are many."

Kovo's eyes glinted. "Illuminate me."

Fel took a steadying breath and then cast about for a moment, looking for props. Finally his eyes settled on one of the many rings he wore. He pried the ring loose and held it up before him.

"Stetriol, my home, is like this gold ring. Rich—beautiful!—all around a circle. But empty on the inside." He closed one eye to gaze through the ring at the colossal ape. "We can grow no crops within the boundaries of the mountains. The flatlands cannot support our settlements. So the land all along our fertile coast grows cramped and polluted." Fel's hands trembled, but not out of fear. The old anger was coming back, and he let it. Anger emboldened him. It made his voice strong, his bearing majestic. "And what happens if enemy ships were to descend upon us?" he continued. "We'd have our backs to the mountains. What happens if a great wave came from the sea to smash us all upon the rocks? My people have nowhere to go."

He placed the ring back onto his finger. "It is my job as king to imagine such nightmare scenarios and to invent solutions for them. And I am very good at half my job."

Kovo made a sound in the back of his throat; it almost sounded like purring. "And the Bile? It would somehow ease your burdens?"

"The Bile?"

"It is why you are here, is it not?"

Feliandor nodded. "There is a song my subjects sing in their taverns. When I first heard it quoted, I thought it was in my honor. 'The good King Fel.'" Fel's face pinched up and his gaze dropped to the ground. "They're saying 'the good king *fell*.' My father, the good king, is gone. And now they're stuck with me." He grasped for the anger, for the fire in his belly that self-pity threatened to suffocate. "I try so hard," he seethed, "and I am hated for trying. Hated for the sin of not being my father. So, yes: The Bile is a gift. It could be a great reward to the faithful. It could make my people hardier, better suited to the harsh realities of our land."

"Perhaps," Kovo said. "But who decides who is worthy of this gift? You? What if that leads only to further resentment? What if they decided to take the Bile from you?"

"They could try," Fel growled.

Kovo laughed, and the sound was like thunder. It dashed Fel's confidence. Here was another situation he was not in control of. What if he had come all this way for nothing?

Then Kovo stepped forward, knuckles first, and Fel's desperation for the Bile was suddenly the least of his concerns. The Great Beast was near enough to crush Fel with his thumb—perhaps with a sneeze. Kovo's breath was hot and rank and it filled the space between them, his massive head blocking out the sun entirely.

Fel fought panic, trying to ignore the realization that he had never been in such immediate danger in his entire life. There had been a dozen guards between him and Griswald; here, he was on his own and at Kovo's mercy.

He held the Great Beast's eyes.

"Your plight moves me," said Kovo at last. "It seems altogether unfair. Such a human invention, unfairness. . . . In nature, the strong dominate, the weak fall, and that is that. But in your . . . *society*, up can so readily become down. Tell me: You are among the five most powerful rulers of your world. Why is it that you should have less than one-fifth of the viable land? Simply due to an accident of birth? It seems to me that you are entitled to more. Just a piece of Nilo, a sliver of Zhong . . . And why not? Would that not be more fair, after all?"

Fel nodded. It hadn't quite occurred to him in those terms. Neither did it occur to him to question or contradict the creature before him.

"And your land is rich with iron," Kovo continued. "So rich that your smiths have more than they know what to do with! It seems to me that arming your people would be a natural use for all that iron."

"My . . . my adviser deemed it unwise to arm the people at a time when they are . . . not content."

"Oh, my, yes, it would be. But not if they had turned their discontent in a direction of your choosing."

"I'm sorry. I don't understand your meaning."

Kovo smiled, showing incisors nearly as long as Fel was tall. "In all the animal kingdom, it is chimpanzees who are the most like humans. And I have always been fond of both species. Do you know how much you have in common?"

Fel's mouth was dry, and he forced himself to swallow. He longed to take a step back, but didn't dare. "We, no, we have no chimpanzees in Stetriol," he said, and felt immediately stupid. Kovo would know that already.

The Great Beast moved again, circling around Fel, along the edge of the clearing. Fel turned in place, determined to keep his eyes on the beast.

"Chimpanzees use tools to accomplish tasks. They solve puzzles and live together in communities." Kovo lifted one massive hand from the ground and gently poked at a nest positioned in the branch of a tree. Baby birds chirped from within.

"And when they do not have enough food," he continued, "they form a raiding party, invade the land of other chimps, and murder their rivals to expand their territory."

Fel saw it coming a second before it happened. Kovo closed his hand around the nest, crushing it, silencing the birdsong with a single violent gesture.

The king stumbled back, clenching his teeth together. He feared what might happen if he screamed.

After a long moment, Kovo turned to look at him. "Simple, no?"

Fel's stomach churned. "You . . . you propose we go to war with our neighbors?"

"War is inevitable in your species, I'm afraid," Kovo purred. "The question is whether your people will go to war with you—*for* you—or against you. Now, do not look so crestfallen. There is plenty of time to turn things around."

"My father spoke of war as a great evil."

"Your father lived in simpler times. That's not really fair either, if you think about it. He left all of Stetriol's problems to you. But I come to you now with solutions. Take the land you deserve. Arm your people with iron and steel . . . and this." Kovo extended the fingers of his other hand, revealing a small vial at the center of his huge black palm.

"Go on," he said, his eyes glinting again.

Feliandor shuffled forward. He reached out slowly, feeling a great trepidation to be so close to so massive a creature. Somehow Kovo's human qualities made his inhumanity all the more striking. Kovo acted like a person, spoke like a person . . . but he was something else entirely. And he could crush Fel in his hand as easily as he had crushed those baby birds.

The Bile was worth the risk. Fel took a deep breath, reached forward, and lifted the vial from Kovo's palm. Kovo smiled, only closing his hand again when Fel had taken three steps back, cradling the vial to his chest the entire time.

"The Bile . . . the bond it brings. It will make me stronger? Faster?"

"The gifts vary from bond to bond. But each bond does bring gifts. And you . . ." Kovo spread his arm out wide. "You have the pick of the litter."

Suddenly the forest was teeming with life. Birds descended from the canopy to flit about just above Fel's head. Rodents burrowed up from the dirt at his feet, and beasts great and small stepped, hopped, and crawled forth from the shrubbery all around him.

Feliandor took a moment to process it all. He felt he had

lost the thread somewhere — lost track of what, exactly, he hoped to accomplish here.

But that was the problem. Feliandor wasn't in control — had not been in control in a long, long time. The Bile was the first step toward imposing some order on all the chaos he'd suffered.

He threw his head back and drank.

The Bile tasted bitter. His head swam, his vision blurred. There was a light — where was it coming from? Then the light was gone, and he was on his knees again. Before him was a crocodile.

"Interesting," Kovo cooed. "I knew this was possible, but it's never happened before. Normally, using the Bile, you would choose an animal to bond with." He flashed his teeth. "But for the first time, you, my king, have summoned a true spirit animal."

Fel was dimly aware of a pressure building in his skull, a headache in bloom. But he could not take his eyes from the crocodile. "You mean — he would have come to me anyway?"

"Yes," said Kovo. "But your bond is different because of the Bile. Thanks to the Bile, you control him. You'll be the one in charge. Your spirit animal will do exactly as you please."

"My spirit animal," Fel echoed. The crocodile was so beautiful, so huge, all lithe muscle and jagged scales. Three times as long as Fel was tall, it looked as if it had been carved out of mossy granite, its greens and browns fading into gray and back again. It appeared strong and ancient, weathered but defiant, as if it had been waiting here, for him, forever.

The island itself seemed to disagree. Noises like screams rang out from the jungle, and what little sunlight there was in the clearing began to fade, though dusk would not come for hours. The mist that hung low to the ground billowed away from the crocodile's formidable bulk, as if afraid to touch it. Fel wasn't afraid.

He reached out and touched its scaly hide.

He felt grounded now. He felt powerful. He looked into its dark, ageless eyes and could believe he was looking into the depths of the night sky. The crocodile opened its jaws wide, displaying rows of deadly teeth. It hissed, but Feliandor didn't flinch.

If appetite was terrible in a king, as Salen had said, how to characterize the appetite of such a fearsome toothed creature as this? It looked big and hungry enough to never be satisfied. It looked fierce enough to devour the world.

And in that moment Feliandor thought: *Well. The world has it coming.*

"Arise, Feliandor," Kovo said for the second time. "Arise, my Reptile King."

There was a great crash from nearby in the forest. The gathered animals all scattered, panicking. The crashing became a rustling; huge trees bent and swayed as if no more than grasses in a breeze.

And then a second Great Beast materialized from the darkness. Gerathon, the Great Serpent. Her full length was lost among the trees, but she drew her hooded head up so that it towered above even Kovo. Where the ape was almost human, Gerathon was a creature from nightmares. Her eyes were flat. Her movements were menacing. There was nothing remotely human in her scaled and fearsome face.

Fel knew that he should be utterly terrified. He knew it, but he didn't feel it.

"We have great plans for you, Feliandor," the monstrous newcomer said. Her forked tongue darted from her mouth as if tasting the air. "The people of Stetriol are going to love the new you."

"No," Feliandor said somberly. "No, I don't think they will." He smiled a wicked smile. "But they will learn to fear me."

Jhi

YIN AND YU

By Billy Merrell

EVERY NIGHT FOR WEEKS, YIN'S LITTLE BROTHER, YU, HAD gotten worse. His mysterious illness had started as a sore throat, but lately the coughs were loud and painful sounding. Enough so that Yin couldn't sleep, afraid for her brother.

A pied starling sat atop his perch in their modest home, a three-bedroom house made of bamboo, clay bricks, and paper. The bird was her spirit animal, Luan, summoned a summer ago. Yin had been the only girl in her village to call a spirit animal in over two years.

Luan was too selfish to be afraid for Yu, but he was kept awake all the same. Every time Yin turned in her bed, the bird would feel the vibration and fly up from his perch, startled. Then he would fluff out his feathers and let out a terrible sound, like a squeaky wagon wheel.

"I'm sorry, Luan," Yin said to the bird, losing her patience. "I can't help it!"

Yin hated Luan as much as she loved him. Starlings were possibly her least favorite bird. Why couldn't she be bonded to a golden pheasant, or a raven, or even a common weaver? Something she could train! Instead she had Luan, who only knew how to complain.

The bird let out another terrible sound. This time, it was because T'ien was hobbling into the room. Something between a bear and a weasel, T'ien was an ancient-looking binturong, a nocturnal animal that crawled around their house at night looking for mice or bugs to eat. T'ien wasn't officially a spirit animal, but he might as well have been. Yin's father had raised T'ien since he was a cub, long before Yin or Yu was born.

Luan puffed up his black and white feathers, but T'ien barely looked up with his cloudy brown eyes. He was on the hunt for something, sniffing the floor. When the binturong slinked into her brother's room, Yin got out of bed. If she wasn't allowed in the room, surely T'ien wasn't either.

She reached to pick up the beast just as it was about to sneak under Yu's bed. She carried T'ien back out the doorway and was about to close the door when she heard her brother call her name.

"Did I wake you?" Yin asked, but Yu shook his head no.

"I can't sleep," he said weakly. The boy was five years old, much younger than Yin, and had always looked up to his big sister. "Will you tell me a story?"

"I only know the one about the storm," she said. "And you've already heard it."

Once, when her brother was little, there was a rain-storm that tore through their village. All night, the wind raced up the mountain they lived on and pulled at their house so that it sounded like the roof was being ripped away, little by little. Yu was scared, and so Yin made up a story about a storm, to make him feel better.

"Please?" Yu begged her. "I'm scared."

"There was a storm," Yin began. "And it came and went, and everyone was okay." She said good night to her brother.

"No," Yu said. "Really tell it."

"Okay, you brat," she said, smiling at the boy with sleepy eyes. She put down T'ien, and the animal scampered away.

"Where should I begin?" she asked him.

"Start in the forest," Yu said, and Yin nodded. But before she could begin the story, Yu started to cough. At first it was gentle, but soon he was coughing so hard that Yin held a rag to his mouth to stifle the sound. When he had finally finished, a little bit of blood came away with the rag.

Yin screamed when she saw it, and her father and mother came rushing into the room. They hurried to Yu's bedside and saw the blood too. Yin's mother picked the boy up in her arms and held him tight to her chest.

"What are you doing in here?" Yin's father asked. "Do you want to get sick too?" He pulled Yin out of the room.

"I want to help," she cried.

"You can't," he said. Hearing that felt scariest of all.

When her mother came from Yu's room, the family agreed it was time to bring the boy back to the village healer. It was a warm night, and the healer's home was only a short journey down the mountain. If they left now, they could reach the healer by sunrise.

"I'm coming too," Yin insisted, but her father hesitated. Finally he agreed. There wasn't time to argue.

All together, they traveled through the dark, carrying Yu in a wooden cart. Luan slept nestled at Yu's side, where Yin would have been if she were allowed in the cart. The road was bumpy, but by sunrise they were knocking on the healer's door.

"Who's there?" asked a woman with a blue sash. Her white hair whipped in the breeze when she opened the door. Immediately she saw the sick boy.

"Nothing you sold us has worked," Yin's father said. "He's getting worse every night!"

The woman looked sad. She stared at the boy with a furrowed brow, and then sighed deeply as she looked up at Yin's parents. Yin studied the woman's face for a sign that her brother would be okay, but all she found there was sorrow.

"No cure is certain. I hope you don't blame the medicine."

"We don't," Yin's mother said. "But we don't have much money left either."

The healer waved for Yin's family to enter. All except for Luan.

"No animals, I'm afraid," the woman said. "I'm sorry."

Luan puffed up defiantly, but before Yin had to ask, the starling blazed onto her skin, just above the girl's wrist.

"Thank you," the woman whispered. With a wink, she lifted her robe to show Yin her own mark. Her spirit animal was a red panda, which slept at her ankle. "You can call me Kuan," the woman told the girl. "And her name is Tzu." She pointed to the tattoo.

"Can I offer anyone some tea?" Kuan said, ushering Yin inside.

"Tea?" Yin's father repeated, sounding furious. "We have walked all night to come here. Can you help us heal my son or not?" Yin had never seen him so scared.

Kuan looked at Yin, then back at her parents.

"There is still hope to be had for your son," Kuan said. "I suggest that we discuss your options in my meditation chamber." Yin's parents stood to follow the woman, and so did Yin.

"Why don't you sit with your brother, dear?" Kuan said, turning back to the girl. "I'm sure he'd like to be with his brave big sister right now."

Yin looked at her mother and father, who nodded solemnly. But Yin didn't feel brave. She knew what the healer was doing. She was leaving Yin out of the conversation, denying her the truth. She wanted to help Yu as badly as they did. Why wouldn't they let her listen?

The three adults passed behind a green curtain, speaking in hushed tones that Yin couldn't make out.

After they were gone, Yin stood by the cart, watching her brother sleep. He looked frail and thin compared to the boy she knew. She wanted to wake him, but Yin knew better. She began to stare at her own tattoo, wondering if Luan felt as alone as she did, or as helpless.

The girl looked around, to make sure no one was

looking. And then she whispered across her skin and summoned Luan. Suddenly the starling leaped from her arm and into the air. Yin didn't care that she was breaking Kuan's rules. She needed to know if her brother would be okay.

Sometimes, playing with Luan, Yin believed she could hear more acutely. She hoped with his help she could listen in from behind the curtain.

Luan took a moment to settle, nestling comfortably on her shoulder. Once he did, Yin spoke in a whisper.

"I need to hear what the healer is saying. Do you think you can help?"

Luan trilled conspiratorially in the girl's ear. Yin closed her eyes tightly, trying her best to block out all other thoughts. Fear kept surfacing, though. Yin could feel her hands shaking at her sides. She pressed her palms together hard to still them, and soon found her center.

Suddenly Yin heard what she thought was a loud wind outside, like a storm was coming. But when she opened her eyes, she saw it was nothing more than a breeze. She knew that it was working; she was drawing on Luan's abilities. But she needed to focus.

Yin closed her eyes again, breathing steadily. Soon she could hear even the quietest sounds in the room. A mosquito landed on a teacup, and to Yin it sounded like a load of firewood set on a table. As she opened her eyes, Yin realized that she was able to hear Kuan's voice from the other room, almost as if she were sitting right beside her.

"There are no guarantees," the healer said, her voice grave.

"Even at that price?!" Yin could hear the outrage in her mother's voice.

"It's an expensive cure, but a powerful one. It's the best I have access to, even at my age," the old woman explained.

"And it's our only option?"

"Of course not," she told them. "There are other healers. Some much more powerful than I am."

"But there's no time!" Yin's mother said. "The next closest healer is a six-day journey through the mountains. Isn't that what you told us when we first came to you?"

"That isn't exactly true," the woman said.

"What is this?" Yin's father said, angry again. Yin could hear the trembling in his voice.

"It's true the closest professional healer is quite far," she said. "The closest practicing *human* healer. But legend has it that the Healthbringer lives in the Great Bamboo Maze that protects us to the south. Her name is Jhi, and she has powers far greater than mine."

"Why would you wait to tell us this?" Yin's father said.

"Because Jhi is beyond our reach," the woman replied. "No one has seen the Great Panda for at least a dozen years. And it's a fool's errand, navigating the Great Bamboo Maze. I wouldn't want to put more of your family in danger."

Yin knew the maze Kuan spoke of. One of the entrances was only a mile south of their home. Her parents had warned her many times to stay away from it. It was rumored to be haunted, though Yin didn't believe that. She did believe, however, that plenty of strong men and women had died inside, from starvation or thirst, their bodies eaten by rats and worms – or by the Maze itself.

Yin's father kept a map of the Maze tucked away in their home. Once, their family had been privy to such important secrets, though Yin doubted the Zhongese military would allow them to keep it now if they knew.

"Tell us more about the Healthbringer," Yin's mother asked Kuan. Yin listened the best she could, but out of the corner of her eye she saw a flash of red that broke her concentration.

She looked up. The curtain swayed lazily, as if something had just passed through it. A small creature leaped onto a shelf behind her, then into the wagon. It was Kuan's red panda, Tzu. The animal's striped tail moved like a cat's, brushing Yu's leg and arm as she walked. Tzu yawned wide, and then curled into a ball at the boy's head and went to sleep.

"Do something!" Yin said to the animal. If Kuan was a healer, maybe her spirit animal was too. "Heal my brother, please."

Tzu opened one of her shiny black eyes to look at Yin. She quickly closed it again, content to sleep.

Yin wanted to scream. Instead Luan flew up into the air, making his terrible squeaky wheel sound, as if to speak for the girl. Yin's father burst from behind the curtain, startling both Yin and Tzu. Luan continued to fly around the room in a panic, so that Yin's father had to duck to dodge the bird.

"Why can't you behave yourself?" Yin's father yelled.

Kuan walked over to the door and held it open until Luan flew outside.

The healer woke Yu. He tried to sit up, but couldn't. His

eyes were crusted and red. Kuan put her hand on the boy's chest as he started coughing. He clenched his jaw between coughs, as if the pain was unbearable. Yu lay back down with a moan, his wet hair stuck to his forehead.

"You have decided, then?" the healer asked Yin's parents. They both nodded, with sorrow in their eyes.

Neither of Yin's parents said a word until they could no longer see Kuan's house.

"What are we going to do?" Yin's mother asked as they climbed the mountain road.

"There's nothing we can do," her father answered. He refused to look at Yin. "I feel horrible about it."

"But what about the cure?" Yin asked. She had heard about a cure.

"It's too expensive," Yin's mother said.

"Besides, it probably won't work," her father added.

"But we have to try!" Yin said.

"We can't afford it. We'd lose the farm. We'd lose everything." Yin's father said it quietly, still refusing to look at her. She could see his bottom lip trembling.

"What about the Sword of Tang?" Yin suggested, but there was no answer from her parents. The ancient sword was the most expensive thing her family owned. In fact, it was priceless.

The sword had been in the family for thousands of years. It carried with it a history of pride and power. Though Yin's family was poor, there was nobility in their blood. Her father had always said that the sword was proof the family would prosper again. The Sword of Tang had its own destiny. One day it would save the family.

"Maybe this is the Sword of Tang's destiny!" Yin offered in a pleading voice.

Her father shook his head. "Out of the question."

"But, Father! How can you be sure?"

"That sword is what gives me my title," he said. "It's what ensures that you'll have a well-born husband one day, and will be taken care of after I'm gone. The Sword of Tang is about the future, Yin, not the present."

"I don't want a husband! I want a brother!" Yin screamed. She had wanted to scream all day. Yin and her brother *were* the future of the family. Didn't that mean that the sword belonged to them?

"When you're older, you'll understand," Yin's mother said. She placed her hand on Yu's back, rubbing it gently.

"I understand now," Yin said, tears filling her eyes. "I want Yu to get better." Yin's mother pulled her close and surprised Yin by beginning to cry herself, in deep sobs. They sounded as painful as Yu's coughing.

Climbing up the mountain road was much harder than traveling down, even in the daylight. By the time their family got home, it was almost evening again, and they were all exhausted. Yin had hoped that during the long journey her mother and father would realize their mistake and consider buying the cure from healer Kuan.

But when they were finally home, Yin's father sent her to bed early with a tone that left no room for argument. It was clear that he had made up his mind.

They were letting her brother die.

That night, Yin listened with Luan for her parents to go to sleep. They waited until T'ien was on the other side of the house, rooting out mice. Then, when they were sure everything was quiet, Yin rose from her bed and crept out of her room, with Luan balanced on her shoulder.

She snuck into her parents' room, matching her steps to the sounds of her father snoring. She moved slowly to the far side of their bed. There, in the center of a small table, was a long parcel wrapped reverently in layers of fine silk.

With only a single glance at her parents' bed, Yin swept the parcel into her hands and moved as quickly as she dared back across the room. Her every step seemed to creak in the tiny, echoing chamber. Right as she was about to reach the door, Yin's father stirred, letting out a loud, surprised grunt. Yin froze.

I've been caught!

But a moment later, he mumbled something quiet and incomprehensible. Yin heard the bed creak behind her as her father rolled over in his sleep.

She moved swiftly from the room, the Sword of Tang clutched in her hands.

"Do you think we're doing the right thing?" Yin asked Luan once they were out in the farmyard, under the moon. It felt like she was asking herself. The little bird flapped his white-and-black wings in the grass, and then flew up to perch on the sword's ancient handle.

Even without being polished, the blade shone in the moonlight.

"Do you remember the way?" Yin asked her spirit animal. Luan flew ahead of the girl, down the mountain road. It was too dark to see clearly, and Yin hadn't thought to bring a torch. The sword already felt heavy in her arms. She labored under its weight, careful not to trip on the stones in the road.

Yin lost track of time as she walked. She had no sense of how much farther she had to carry the sword in secret. She refused to rest until she absolutely could not take another step. Finally that moment came, and Yin collapsed onto the ground. She sat there in the dark with Luan, listening to the forest.

"Do you ever wish you were without me?" she asked the starling. "Do you wish you'd been bonded to some other girl, with a better life?" She didn't expect him to answer her, but the bird opened his beak and let out a sweet song. Yin had only heard his screams, his whines, the terrible sounds Luan made to get her attention. She had never heard him sing so splendidly. It filled her heart with hope. She knew she was doing the right thing.

Yin got up and started walking again. She was ready to be brave, even if her parents weren't.

When Yin arrived at the healer's village, it was still late. There were many hours left before daybreak. Yin knew it wasn't safe traveling alone this late at night. She had the sword to protect her, but she was too weak and untrained to wield it properly. If anyone found the girl alone in the dark, they could easily steal it. Then Yin would have nothing. She had to be careful.

Luan flew ahead of Yin, her brave scout. And yet with every step, Yin felt like she might be walking into a trap. She imagined that she was hearing voices, men and women in the shadows plotting to charge her. She looked behind her, into the dark. No one was there. And yet it sounded like people were running toward her.

When she faced forward, Luan flew back to her. It was starting to rain. First gently, and then all at once. Rainwater filled the streets with mountain mud. Her dress was getting muddier with every step.

It would be obvious to Yin's parents that she'd betrayed them, but it was too late to turn back. She had come too far, and all on her own.

Yin knocked at Kuan's door, and Luan let out an impatient squawk. As they waited, Yin asked Luan to sleep again on her arm. The bird bristled with indignation. He flew to her outstretched arm, but instead of doing as Yin asked, Luan pecked at her skin defiantly.

"Ouch!" Yin cried, startled. "That pinches!"

Luan cried out too, but did as Yin asked, disappearing in a blur of motion.

Kuan opened the door wide, as if she had been expecting the girl all along. In her hand was a large lit candle.

"You're very brave indeed," the healer told Yin.

"I've come to buy Yu's cure," she told the woman, revealing the Sword of Tang. Kuan leaned in with the candle, and the wet sword glimmered like the hungry flame.

"My child," Kuan said, "this sword is much too valuable to trade. I could never accept such a prize as payment."

"But you must," Yin begged her. "It's all I have."

"Your father could not have allowed it," Kuan said.

"It's my sword to give, not his," the girl protested.

Kuan stared at her a long while with steady eyes. Yin had heard about the healer's gaze, that the woman was a master at intuiting what was inside a person. But Yin was telling the truth, so she stared right back.

"I will sell you my strongest cure," the woman told Yin, "and will take your sword as payment for it. I will keep it safe for you. Perhaps one day you'll come back for it. I'll return it to you then, for a fair price."

"You are an honorable woman," Yin said to Kuan. Tzu, the healer's red panda, climbed up the woman's arm and perched like a monkey on her shoulder, his striped tail curling behind her neck.

"Not nearly as honorable as you are courageous," Kuan said, handing Yin a small vial of dark liquid. It coated the glass, thick as blood.

"Thank you!" Yin said, hugging the old woman. "A million times, thank you."

Kuan frowned at the girl's delighted face. "What's in that bottle is a chance, not a miracle," she warned. "His fever will break by morning, or not at all."

But it felt like a miracle to Yin. She turned from the door, ready to run home to her brother before morning.

"Be sure to tell your parents what I said," the healer called behind her. "As long as I am alive, the Sword of Tang will be waiting here for you."

Yin gripped the vial hard in her fist and ran through the rain, out of the village and up the mountain road. She was no longer scared of robbers, or of tripping on stones. She felt like she herself could fly, spry as her spirit animal, dodging the raindrops. She would have sung, if she weren't using every breath in her body to get her home.

Yin was soaked to the bone when she arrived home, the vial hot in her hand. She rushed into her brother's room and woke him, her hair still dripping down her face.

"Drink this," she said, uncorking the potion and holding it to the boy's dry lips. "You should be better by breakfast," she told him.

"It smells," Yu said, but he drank Kuan's cure in one gulp. He coughed and then put his hand to his chest, like he felt something working inside. Yin smiled, hoping it was the medicine.

"Sleep now," Yin said to her brother. Yu kissed his sister on her cold cheek. He lay back down and closed his eyes, sniffling but smiling.

Yin watched him for a long time before she changed out of her wet clothes and crept into her warm, dry bed. She considered waking Luan, just to say good night, and to thank him for being such a brave companion. But she fell asleep as soon as the thought crossed her mind.

The next morning, Yin woke to the sound of T'ien snarling. It was a high-pitched sound the binturong usually made when he was hungry. But she soon realized what had really upset T'ien.

Her father was tearing through the house, looking for the Sword of Tang. Yin heard the commotion as teacups fell from the cupboard shelves, breaking on the floor.

"Where is it?!" Yin's father yelled.

Yin jumped out of bed to check on her brother. Kuan had told her that if the cure worked, Yu's fever would break by morning. Now the sun was up, and Yu hadn't coughed for hours.

"How do you feel?" Yin asked, looking down at her brother. He gazed up at her through bleary eyes.

Yu shook his head and frowned, then put his hand up to his throat. He opened his mouth and moved his lips, like he was trying to speak, only no sound came out.

"Your voice is gone?" Yin asked. Her brother nodded. She put her hand to his forehead.

He was burning hot! Yu's fever was worse than she'd thought possible.

"This can't be. It has to work!" Yin said. But even as she spoke the words, she knew that she was wrong. Kuan had warned her of this. There were no guarantees.

Yin covered her face and cried quietly, not wanting her parents to hear. She wanted to hide, to run away. It was bad enough that her brother was dying; now Yin had gambled her family's title away. She'd made things worse. She didn't know how she could face her father or mother, having disobeyed their wishes. She'd lost the Sword of Tang. She might as well die right there with her brother.

Yu was looking at Yin like he wanted to say something.

"What is it?" Yin asked, hoping he could somehow answer her.

Yu put his hands together, like he was praying. Then he opened them, as if opening a book.

"You want me to tell you a story?" Yin asked, and her brother nodded.

"I walked all night through the rain," she told Yu. "I don't want to tell that story. I'm sorry." But her brother looked so sad. She wondered what it must feel like, not getting to leave his bed, knowing that he might die without taking another step. She pictured Yu walking in the rain with a smile on his face, enjoying every sensation.

"There is a new story I heard," she told him, and his face lit up. "About a healer they call the Healthbringer. Her name is Jhi. She's a giant panda, and she lives in a maze made entirely of bamboo." Yu smiled for the first time in weeks.

Yin heard her father calling for her from outside. She didn't feel ready to face him. Maybe she wouldn't ever be. Not until Yu was cured.

Suddenly an idea struck her.

"Do you want to come with me to the Maze?" she asked her brother. "We will go to meet Jhi and ask her to heal you."

Yu nodded and tried to sit up, but he was too weak. Yin would have to carry him. She tied her dress in a knot and hung it over her shoulder like a sling. She pulled her brother up to her chest and into the sling. She crept from her brother's room into the main chamber of the house, grateful that her father was now searching for her outside. It didn't take long for her to find the old family map of the Great Bamboo Maze.

Soon she was running out the door, her father calling after her in the fields.

Yu's skin felt hot to the touch. He gulped in the fresh air and then immediately started to cough.

"Jhi is going to be so happy to meet you," Yin told her brother. She hoped that she was right.

The Maze was an incredible thing to behold from the inside. Ancient bamboo stalks stood twice as tall as Yin's house, filling the path in front of the girl with rustling shadows. Almost as soon as Yin had entered, all sound seemed muted against the gentle swaying of the thick stalks and their high, distant leaves.

As they walked, Yin told her brother everything she had heard about Jhi the healer, little as it was, as well as every story she'd been told about the Great Bamboo Maze—which turned out to be quite a few.

Yin had been carrying Yu for a long time, and her legs were already sore. She stopped at a crossroads in the bamboo to check her map. She summoned Luan, who sprang from the girl's skin as if from a cage, only to find himself surrounded by bamboo. He hopped along the dirt path, making his terrible noise.

"We should be here," Yin said, ignoring him and pointing to a pin in the fabric of the map. The bamboo walls were marked with crossed green threads. She'd been careful to keep track of where they were in the Maze.

The starling flew up and surveyed their surroundings from the air. When he landed again, he seemed even more agitated. Luan hopped along the map's edges angrily. He pecked at the fabric, tearing at the edges in tiny bites. Then he pulled some of the green threads until they broke away.

"You're ruining it!" Yin shouted, frantically shooing

the bird away with her hands. "Is this because I took too long to summon you?"

Luan had pulled out a whole line of green Xs.

"This is where we are. I'm certain," Yin said, and the bird nodded.

"You're so annoying!" she said.

Yin's back was to a wall of bamboo, but according to the map the wall was very thin. Yin had planned to take the long way around, walking with Yu half a mile or more, simply to turn and walk half a mile back on the other side.

"Do you think I'm small enough to pass through the bamboo?" she said to Luan. If she could manage it, she would save them a mile of walking. When Luan didn't answer her, she stood up and decided to try.

Yin looked deep into the copse of bamboo. Each stem was thicker than the girl's arm, but they bent when she shoved them. She pushed until there was a gap between the stems, and then stepped onto one of the reeds. She weighed just enough so that the plants didn't break, and instead held her there off the ground. She took a step with the other foot. Again, the bamboo supported her.

Suddenly there was a crashing sound, as if the bamboo around her was breaking all at once. Yin leaped back just in time, as the stalks cracked apart. She covered her brother as a few of the poles toppled toward them.

Once it was quiet again, Yin looked into the hole she'd made. Down on the ground, at root level, something was sticking out of the soil. It looked like an animal trap, with jagged metal teeth. Yin's weight must have triggered the jaws to close. If she hadn't leaped back, she would have fallen right into the trap.

"I won't try that again," she said to Luan.

Yin looked at her brother sleeping soundly despite the crashing of the bamboo. For a second, it looked like he had some color in his cheeks. But Yin realized it was only the sunset, turning everything pink before the evening set in.

Yin wanted to get as deep into the Maze as she could before nightfall. She pressed on, carrying her brother half a mile, to where there was an opening in the wall. Yin took out her map.

"Luan!" she said, finally understanding what the bird had been doing. "You fixed it! The map was wrong, and you fixed it!" She looked to where the Xs had been removed, and there in the dirt were the roots of bamboo shoots that had been torn away.

"Is anything else wrong?" she asked. Luan flew up into the purple sky to survey the bamboo again. When he landed, he looked hard at the stitches. After long consideration, he started to peck at another line of marks. Once those were gone, he pecked at others. Yin started to question the starling's work again. Either the bird was wrong, or the map was uselessly out of date.

The last of the daylight was disappearing. Soon, Yin couldn't read the map at all. In her hurry to leave, she hadn't thought to bring a torch or candle. She sat in the darkness, feeling sorry for herself.

Though Yin couldn't see the map clearly in the dark, she could still feel the stitches, and where some Xs had been removed.

The Maze is changing, she thought. *Why else would the map be wrong?*

She pictured a team of workers digging up the Maze, moving whole walls of bamboo out, pole by pole. It seemed like an impossible task. Each gap of bamboo removed was as large as a house. It would take a lot of workers to dig all that up.

Yin looked into the night sky. She couldn't see the moon, but a great many stars twinkled like silver pebbles in a dark lake. She heard a rustling in the high leaves and remembered what she'd heard about the Maze being haunted. Yin closed her eyes tightly and listened, unaided by her spirit animal. The wind made it sound like there were people all around her in the bamboo, on every side. At least, she hoped it was the wind.

Suddenly something moved next to the girl. It wasn't Luan or her brother, but something else that darted beside her in the shadows. The hair on Yin's neck stood up as she held her breath to listen. This time Luan lent her some of his skill, and together they heard everything.

Tiny feet scampered in the dirt. Mouths gnawed the young shoots across the path. There were rats all around her, nesting in the bamboo. The rodents roved together through the night-dark paths, eating anything they could.

Yu let out an unpleasant moan, and Yin realized one of the filthy animals had nosed its way into the sling with her brother. Luan screeched loudly, and the rat scampered away. Yin pulled her brother tight to her chest and let out a worried gasp. His skin felt like it was on fire.

Every night for many nights, Yu's illness had only gotten worse. Why would Yin think a night in the Great Bamboo Maze would be any different? She stared at the stars, asking them quietly to guide her. Yin had often wished on stars, but not like she did that night. She gazed at them as Luan nestled into her, until it didn't feel like she was talking to stars anymore. The two brightest shone like silver eyes in a dark face, listening to Yin's prayer.

Exhausted from her journey, Yin gave herself over to the sounds of bamboo and the face in the night sky. Slowly, a peace came over her.

In her dreamy state, Yin realized why the Maze was changing.

She imagined a giant panda, as big as a house. She pictured her wandering through the Maze, sitting to snack in the shade. It wouldn't take long for a panda that big to leave a sizable dent in a bamboo wall. Yin decided that must be why some of the bamboo had disappeared, why the map was no longer correct.

Jhi was here.

Yin smiled at Luan after she thought it. The bird was onto something. If Yin could follow what Jhi had eaten, maybe it would lead her to the Great Panda. Maybe she could save her brother after all.

The next morning, Yu's illness was worse. It was just as Yin had feared. She was certain her brother would not make it through another night. They were out of time. She had to track down Jhi today if there was any hope for Yu.

Luan flew above to scout a path. When he returned, he hopped along the edges of the map as Yin flattened the fabric out. Luan looked serious, his dark eyes scanning the fabric. Suddenly the bird flapped his wings, excited.

"What is it?" Yin asked him. Luan pecked at the cloth, touching one of the green threads several times with his beak before tearing it loose. "That bamboo was there yesterday . . ." the girl said, and the bird nodded his tiny head. Luan then flew up to lead the way.

Yin picked up her brother. He groaned, but Yin couldn't tell if Yu was sleeping or awake. His eyes were barely open, and even his breathing sounded painful.

"You're going to be okay," Yin promised her brother. Then she hurried to follow Luan's lead, carrying the sick boy as fast as she could through the Maze.

Yin kept the map handy as she walked, occasionally checking to see where Luan had led them. It wasn't long before they were approaching a major crossroads. The girl looked down at the map. Three different paths converged at the one spot ahead of Yin. And beyond it, up one of the paths, was where Jhi had eaten.

Yin began to walk quickly, but then she heard a sound that stopped her in her tracks.

Voices. There was a sound, like someone opening and closing the latch on a box. Yin paused to listen. There were three or four men somewhere in the bamboo. She didn't know what they were working on, but they talked as if they were taking great care.

Yin looked up. She could see the tops of the leaves moving, and not from the wind. One patch of bamboo specifically was shaking. Suddenly there was a clang, and the workers gave relieved sighs, as if they'd finished something very difficult. Or dangerous.

The girl looked again at her map. She could see that the bamboo walls dividing the path were much narrower as they approached the crossroads. The men's voices were coming from the other side of the wall. But what were they doing?

Yin leaned into the bamboo and listened closely. Luan flew back to aid her.

"Jhi has been here," one man said. "This patch. It looks like she's been eating here, doesn't it?"

"How would you know?" another said.

"If she stops to eat here again, she'll have a surprise waiting for her," a third voice said. It sounded like a much younger person, a boy not much older than Yin.

Yin remembered the trap she'd encountered earlier in the Maze. It was deep in the bamboo itself. Maybe these men had put the trap there. But why? To catch Jhi?

All along, Yin had felt like an outsider in the Great Bamboo Maze. She was searching for Jhi, as if the Maze belonged to the Great Beast. But now these men were talking about the panda as if *she* were the outsider. It seemed like they wanted Jhi for some reason.

Yin didn't know what the group of men wanted for sure, but she knew she had to find Jhi before they did. If they caught the panda, there would be no hope for curing Yu.

Suddenly her brother coughed.

Yin whispered for the boy to be quiet. She felt his forehead. Yu was sweating, and yet his lips looked dry and chapped. He coughed again, more loudly. Yin worried the sound would alert the workers.

She listened.

"Whoever it is, we'll get them," the men were saying. She could hear they were already running her way. She looked at the map. There were bends and curves on their side of the bamboo wall. If the map was right, it would take them a while to get to her. Still, she had to hurry.

Yin ran for the crossroads as fast as she could, her brother coughing painfully the whole way. As she burst into the sunlight, it momentarily blinded her. Luan flew straight for the path to where Jhi had eaten, but Yin couldn't see which way he'd taken.

Yin felt someone watching her.

She turned around, and a black boar stepped into the sunlight, peering toward her. It snorted and stomped the ground. The girl began to back away, staring in horror at the boar's sharp tusks and angry eyes.

Suddenly there was a growl so deep it felt like the ground was shaking. The sound made Yin's blood turn cold in her veins. She turned and saw a white-and-green alligator poke its long snout into the sun behind her. The reptile opened its wide jaws, hissing at the girl.

Each of the beasts would have been a frightening sight on their own. Together, they made Yin wonder if she was in a nightmare: lost in a maze with dangerous predators. Something told her it wasn't a coincidence that both of these animals had come upon her.

Out of the bamboo came three of the men Yin had heard. Only they weren't dressed like workers. They were dressed like warriors, soldiers – but for whose army? Yin didn't recognize their foreign uniforms. These men were not part of Zhong's military. So who were they?

The black boar circled back to a man in a gray cloak. The alligator whipped its tail back and forth, then backed behind a pale man with red hair. The men looked at Yin as if they didn't know what to do with her.

"Don't move," the red-haired man commanded. Yin froze. Where was Luan when she needed him most? She imagined him watching the scene from a safe perch, high up in the canopy of the bamboo.

Two more men emerged, along with a boy.

"Who is this?" the boy said. Yin recognized his voice from before. He had a spirit animal too. An orange-and-white dhole, as wild-looking as any dog Yin had seen on the mountain. The animal snarled when it saw Yin, gnashing its teeth.

"Grab her," someone said, and Yin ran. Out of the corner of her eye, she saw Luan, flapping his white-and-black wings. She ran toward the bird, down the path he was motioning from.

Yin had never run faster than she did right then, even though she was carrying her small brother, and nearly tripping on the dirt below her feet. At some point she turned back to look, but none of the animals or soldiers had followed her.

Yin noticed that the bamboo around her was different than she'd seen. Dark and old. She could see spiderwebs in the shadows at the base of the bamboo.

"Luan," Yin whispered. Her legs were beginning to feel weak and clumsy. "Don't lose me."

Suddenly the starling flew back to her from ahead. Yin could tell the bird was nervous. The bamboo that formed the Maze was unhealthy looking here; the leaves and stalks were spotted with gray mold. When Yin saw it, she checked the map. She didn't believe Jhi would eat diseased bamboo. Luan flew up high to check their position. Sure enough, they were headed the right way. In fact, the starling eagerly ripped another X from the map. It seemed Jhi had eaten even more bamboo since that morning.

"What would I do without you?" the girl asked her spirit animal. Luan fluffed his feathers and let out a small song. Then, with pride swelling in his chest, he turned to fly ahead again.

As soon as Luan was in the air, though, something pounced. What had looked to Yin like nothing more than a shadow leaped out of the dark bamboo at Luan, pinning the bird to the ground. Yin screamed. It was a bird spider, a tarantula. The hairy arachnid was as big as Yin's head. The spider hadn't bitten Luan, not yet. But why was it waiting?

Out of the far shadows stepped a woman in the same uniform as the men Yin had run from. The woman was old. She didn't look like a soldier, and anyway, Zhong's military didn't allow female warriors. She smiled a devilish smile, revealing rows of black, rotted teeth.

Yin stepped back as the woman approached her. The woman reached down and grabbed Luan with both hands, and as she did the spider climbed up the woman's arm and neck, into her nest of hair. It perched on the top of the woman's head, fluffing her hair with its eight thick legs.

"Give him back!" Yin demanded.

"The Great Bamboo Maze is no place for children," the woman said, looking down at Yu asleep in the sling. Yin could barely carry her brother anymore. She was so tired. Too tired to run. But she stood straight as she addressed the woman in front of her on the path.

"I need to find the Healthbringer, Jhi," Yin told her. "My brother is sick."

"I can see that," the woman said, a small smile on her face. She checked behind her and over Yin's shoulders before whispering, "I want to help you. Perhaps if you just come with me . . ."

Yin's mouth fell open. She didn't understand.

The woman held Luan out to Yin, but when the girl reached for the bird, the woman grabbed her wrist, right where Luan went when he slept as a tattoo. Soon she was dragging Yin up the path, back toward the men and animals at the crossroads.

"Who are you?" Yin asked the woman, sobbing. "Why are you doing this?"

"I'm going to help you," the woman said. "And you are going to help us." Then she snatched Yu's sling from her. Yin cried out in protest, but the old woman was stronger than she appeared, forcing her down. Soon she was carrying the sick child herself and pulling Yin behind her.

They arrived at a ragged camp filled with soldiers like the ones Yin had encountered earlier. Most were just sitting around waiting to be given orders. One of them hailed the old woman, calling her Nao. Strangely, every one of the soldiers appeared to have a spirit animal. Yin had always heard that the Marked were very rare.

The old woman pushed Yin forward, and she fell face-first into the dirt.

"Get this brat to work," Nao snapped at her fellow soldiers. "There are more traps to be made. I want that oafish panda's talisman in my hands before the invasion begins."

"What are you going to do with Jhi once you find her?" Yin asked, wiping dirt from her face, but she received no answer. Instead, one of the soldiers tossed her a uniform like everyone else's.

"If we find her, can I ask the panda a question?" Yin called after the woman as she walked away with Yu. *"Please!"* she begged.

Nao just ignored her.

Yin was forced to set up traps in the bamboo for the rest of the afternoon, metal jaws that sprang closed when triggered. Since her arms were long and slender, the old woman had insisted the girl would be better at maneuvering around the trigger. But Yin knew it was the most dangerous job. That was why Nao had her do it.

Yin remembered Kuan's face as she had told Yin she was brave. But the longer she worked, the less brave she felt. The day turned into the early evening, and soon the sky grew dusky.

Yin's hopes for her brother were dashed. She was certain that he wouldn't make it another night without Jhi's healing. Now it was nearly dark, and there was no panda to speak of.

Nao had Yin set one last trap in the dimming light. The girl's hand shook uncontrollably as she reached in the dark between the trap's strong jaws and past the metal trigger. She wondered if the traps could hurt the Great Panda. Yin worried what would happen to her brother if Jhi was killed. Or if she were.

Finished with their work for the night, the soldiers disappeared into their tents. Yin had no tent but didn't care where she slept, so long as she was with Yu, who had been laid in the middle of the camp. Nao returned Luan to Yin before she herself retired, tossing the terrified bird at her. She also gave Yin a half-filled skin of water, barely enough for her and her brother. Yin made sure Yu drank it all, though it stung his throat to swallow.

"I promised you a story, didn't I?" Yin asked the boy once they were alone. It made him smile, as it always had. She wanted to remember her brother smiling.

"There once was a storm," Yin said. "It wasn't anyone's fault. It just happened."

Yu grinned weakly at his big sister. The sight brought tears to her eyes.

"The storm came and swept over the village. It blew shingles off the roofs of houses. It plucked flags from the flagpoles and tore shutters off of windows." Yin watched her brother's eyes twinkle. They were so bright, it looked like the moon was full in the sky. But when Yin looked up, the sky was cloudy.

Usually, when Yin told the story, she said it all with a happy voice. She described the shrill wind and the echoing thunder. She made Yu laugh with how loudly and lively she'd tell it. It wasn't really about the story, it was how she told it to her brother that made him like it.

But Yin was sad that night, and her heart was too heavy to tell it the way he wanted. Yu seemed too tired to care which version she told. He was simply happy to hear her speak.

"A bucket on the porch filled with rainwater," she said. "And then the wind blew all the rain out until the bucket was dry. And then the storm filled the bucket up again.

All night the porch shook and lightning crashed."

Yin glanced down. It looked like her brother was sleeping. He seemed peaceful, at least. She watched his chest, relieved every time he took a breath, until she couldn't watch anymore, afraid that if she continued, her brother's breathing might stop.

"But in the morning, it was gone," Yin said. "All the wind and the rain. All the shaking and the echoes and the crashing. And everything in the village was peaceful again. And everyone was okay. Everyone."

Yin began to cry again. This time, though, her tears weren't those of fear. They were of acceptance. She knew her brother couldn't continue like he had.

"You're so brave," Yin told her little brother. "Have I said that? I'm so very proud to be your sister." One last time, Yu smiled. And then he closed his eyes again, as if to sleep.

"Good night," Yin said. "I love you."

She lay down on the path, looking up at the cloudy sky. The bamboo swayed high above her, and her vision blurred with each new tear. It was as if new shadows were darkening the highest leaves. But when Yin looked, it wasn't darkness she saw, but light. She saw two silver stars, and remembered them from the night before.

Were they really so bright that they could shine through the clouds? Yin wasn't sure, but she stared into them. She tried so hard to be at peace with her brother dying. But she couldn't be. She wasn't ready. She thought of her parents and how they'd lost everything because of her – their son and daughter and title. Their whole future.

Still, a calm overtook Yin's body, as it had the night

before. Suddenly Yin felt like she understood everything around her. She could hear every soldier in his tent, sleeping or trying to sleep. She could see in the dark, even the ill-lit details of the strangers' camp.

Luan flashed unbidden onto Yin's skin, just above her wrist. Yin felt a power overtake her. It was like when she accessed Luan's gifts, only she knew that wasn't it. She listened deep into the bamboo. She heard the distant rats and closer spiders in their bamboo webs. She didn't feel sore anymore. In fact, she suddenly felt like she had slept for days.

Yin whispered to her brother.

"I'm going to find Jhi," she told him, "and bring her back to you."

Yin didn't know if she would find the panda, but she had to try. Mysteriously, she felt like she could.

She snuck out of camp without waking a single soldier. And then quickly, a plan appeared in her mind. She knew how the traps worked. What if she turned their own traps against them? Yin knew she would have to work quickly and quietly to turn every trap she'd set against the soldiers. But it would be worth it in the morning if the army suddenly found themselves triggering their own weapons.

But could she do it? Yin felt sure that she could. She felt she could do anything right then. It was as if the night had slowed down around her.

Yin approached each trap calmly. They seemed simple now, and somehow she could remember every trap site, even some she didn't help assemble. It was as if they were all written down on a map in her mind.

Yin worked quickly, until she finished resetting the last of the traps. Finally, when she'd finished, Yin closed her eyes to listen. She believed if she listened hard enough, she'd hear the great Jhi shuffling lazily through the dark. But instead, as she listened, the sounds all muddled together. The clarity she'd found was gone.

Just then, Yin heard a snap, like a stalk of bamboo cracking behind her.

When she turned, she expected to see Nao in her uniform, or another soldier, come to bring her back to the camp. Instead, she saw what looked like a large shadow filling the path. She looked up at the huge creature. A panda, many times the size of any that Yin had ever heard of or seen, sat down with a crunch in front of the girl.

Jhi looked at Yin with curiosity. Silently, the two regarded each other, the huge panda and the little girl. Glittering at Jhi's throat was a silver chain, and on it a carved green figure that shined as if it were lit from within. The panda saw the girl staring at the talisman and covered it quickly with her huge paw.

There was a loud clap and a scream in the distant bamboo. The sound was followed by another. The traps were going off.

"They're coming!" Yin warned Jhi, but the panda didn't look at all worried.

"They want to hurt you!" the girl said. "You have to run!" But Jhi just sat there.

All around them, the soldiers began to appear. First the redheaded man with the alligator, followed by the others. Finally Nao appeared, her spider leaping off her arm toward the girl.

Yin cried out, afraid. But all of a sudden the soldiers were moving slowly, as if they were underwater. Yin looked up at Jhi. The panda didn't seem fazed. One by one the soldiers lay down against the bamboo and fell asleep. Their animals slept too, some disappearing into marks on the soldiers' skin. After a moment, only the tarantula and Nao were left standing, creeping toward Jhi on opposite sides.

"I don't want to hurt you," Jhi said, her voice full and lovely.

"You can't," Nao snarled. The woman feinted left, and as Jhi lifted herself up to follow, the tarantula leaped up and snatched the carved green talisman. Yin could only watch as, in a second, the spider scampered up the panda's neck, pulling the precious object away from Jhi, chain and all. In an instant, both Nao and the tarantula were gone, running down the path and into the Maze, faster than Yin thought possible. Nao screeched with laughter as the spider trailed behind her.

The Great Panda seemed conflicted. Her sad eyes followed the woman into the dark.

"Why didn't you stop her?" Yin asked Jhi, knowing the Great Beast had great powers.

The panda turned her attention back to Yin.

"Because you need me more, right now."

Jhi leaned her enormous head toward Yin, who screamed in surprise at the sight of the beast's toothy grin. Yin felt a wet, warm surface pass over her palms, and watched in awe as Jhi pulled back, the panda's giant pink tongue receding back into her mouth.

Yin looked at her palms. They weren't blistered or sore anymore. *It must have been Jhi's magic*, she thought. The girl looked up into Jhi's eyes, big and silver on the panda's face. The eyes seemed familiar to Yin. Too familiar.

Suddenly the girl understood what she was looking at.

"You've been following me!" Yin said to Jhi accusingly. "This whole time, you've been watching. That first night, that was you, wasn't it?"

Jhi blinked silently. The panda's huge face blocked out the early morning light, so that only her silver eyes shone high above the girl. They looked like silver stars twinkling.

"Who are these soldiers?" Jhi finally asked. Her voice was rich and calm, like a thousand bamboo leaves rustling in the hushed wind. "Who was that woman who took my talisman?"

Yin told the Healthbringer everything she knew: They had set traps and intended to catch Jhi. But as Yin explained it, she remembered her brother, who she'd left at the soldiers' camp.

"You were with me the whole time?!" Yin asked Jhi again. This time she was angry. "Why did you let my brother get sicker? *Why did you leave him to die?*" Yin pictured her brother now, alone in the camp, his body cold and still.

"How could you?" Yin asked Jhi.

But the panda had other things on her mind.

"I must contact the others," Jhi said, rising slowly. "Humans are hunting our talismans."

"Wait," Yin demanded, but the panda continued, as slow as a glacier in the dark morning.

"I needed you to prove yourself," Jhi said to the girl. "And you did just that." But Yin didn't understand. What had she proven?

"Yin?" A voice echoed in the reeds, barely more than a breeze. Yin's breath caught in her throat. She recognized that voice.

Yu emerged from the shadows beyond Jhi. He looked dangerously thin from his illness, but the boy could walk and talk. And he was smiling.

"Oh, Yu!" Yin exclaimed, running to hold him. "Thank you, Jhi! Oh, thank you!"

Luan flashed out from Yin's wrist. At the sight of Yu safe and sound, he began flying in circles around the boy.

The panda didn't look back at them. Instead, she walked on, deeper into the Great Bamboo Maze.

"Please!" Yin called after her. "Let me repay you, Healthbringer! If there's any way I can be of use to you, I would like nothing more than to help you, if I can."

The panda stopped as she considered the girl's offer. "There may be something you can do. I think the time will come soon when those with gifts such as yours will be needed. I will take you and your brother home. After a week, I would like you to return to me, if you are willing. There is great trouble ahead. You will hear it more clearly than others. Will you lend me your aid?"

"Anything," Yin told the legendary animal.

Without another word, Jhi lowered her paw before Yin. The girl stepped on top and was lifted with her brother high onto the Great Panda's back. And then Jhi continued on her way, carrying both of them to safety, and whispering more warnings of the dangers to come.

Zhong soon fell to a surprise attack from its neighbor, Stetriol—an act that began the first great war with the Devourer. In the years after Feliandor was finally defeated, Yu grew up to become a renowned storyteller. He spent his life recounting the exploits of the green-cloaked heroes who fought to liberate Zhong from the Devourer's army. But his favorite story was always of his older sister, Yin. Though the armies of Zhong forbade women from fighting, she had wielded the mighty Sword of Tang countless times defending her home. She was the finest spy the green-cloaked resistance had in occupied Zhong, and the bravest woman he'd ever known.

Uraza

THE FIRST
GREENCLOAK

By Gavin Brown

VIOLET EYES GLEAMED IN THE DARK. THE ENORMOUS CAT
glided under red acacia trees, a shadow outlined
by dim moonlight. Uraza sniffed the wind. The scent of
prey was on the air. But it was not the antelopes, deer, or
wildebeests that she hunted for food. No, this was the ugly
scent of men, polluting her hunting grounds with their
stink. Filling her peaceful night with their coarse songs
and flickering fires. Waddling across her lands with their
ungainly two-legged walk.

Uraza was twice the height of a normal leopard, with
blinding speed and the ferocity of a tornado. She was not
just a normal predator. She was a Great Beast, one of the
fifteen who had walked Erdas since the earliest days.

She crested a hill, looking down across the savanna at the small group clustered around a campfire. More foreigners, with their metal helmets and swords, and their destructive habits. The predators of Nilo had learned to stay clear of her hunting grounds. Only thick, prideful men insisted on straying in. Generally the locals honored her, showing her the respect and admiration due a Great Beast. But even they had become more insolent in recent days.

A delegation of elders from the eastern villages had come last week, begging for her assistance. "Great Uraza, beauteous queen of the savanna," their leader had entreated her. "Please help us fight these foreigners. They attacked without warning, betraying many years of peace. We need your aid to drive them from Nilo."

Uraza had snarled at them, chasing them across the river marking the boundary of her hunting grounds. Who did they think she was? One of their village dogs, to be ordered around when they needed her? One of their precious spirit animals, to be forced into a life of cohabitation with them? This was just a conflict between two human tribes. And humans needed to deal with their own problems. Let them appeal to a soft-hearted Great Beast like Ninani, who enjoyed meddling in everyone else's business.

All Uraza cared about was that none of them entered her hunting grounds. The camp below her had been made in her territory, so those humans would pay. She prowled forward, her keen ears picking up their conversation as she advanced.

"Samilia ordered us to scout out the hunting grounds. I'd rather be ripped up by a giant leopard than come back to her empty-handed," one of them was saying.

"I heard stories at the last village," another one answered. "She's massive and vicious. She doesn't even let the locals enter. They say she's so large that she can eat a man in two bites. If we go in there, we're as good as dead."

Uraza's teeth gleamed in the darkness as she smiled. Perhaps that one would be suffered to live, if only to spread tales of her glory to the rest of the foreigners. The huge cat waited a moment, until the watchman posted at the edge of the firelight looked away. Then she charged forward. He turned back and stared at her in slack-jawed shock as she rocketed into the light of the fire. He went down with one swipe of her claws.

The night erupted in screams and shouts. Some of the soldiers panicked, but others grabbed swords and shields and advanced on her. Uraza simply laughed, a deep rumble booming across the savanna. She leaped at them, extending her claws and batting aside the steel as they swung it. One she raked across the face with her claws, another she sent careening with a thrust from her shoulder.

Uraza crashed through the camp, slashing tents and sending pots and pans falling into the mud.

"Please!" one of the soldiers said, throwing up his hands in surrender as she bore down on him. Uraza leaned in close, able to smell the fear that she saw in his wide eyes. She snarled, using a single claw to draw a cut across his chest.

"Go," she rumbled at the pathetic man. "Cross the river, and leave my hunting grounds forever. Tell your people that anyone else who enters my borders will end their journey in my belly."

The man nodded, face completely drained of color.

"Now go!" Uraza roared.

The man fled into the night, immediately followed by his companions. She heard them stumbling through the dark long after she could no longer see them. Uraza kicked a massive clod of dirt onto the fire and slipped back into the night.

Half an hour later, she sniffed the air and growled with satisfaction. The stink of humans no longer clung to the air.

For the next week, Uraza thought that the foreigners had learned their lesson. The sweet smell of distant fires reached her when the breezes blew westward, but no humans violated her borders. Then, on the ninth day, as she stalked a herd of gazelles across the grassy highveld, Uraza's nose once again caught the smell of invaders on the wind. She reluctantly turned from her prey and made her way down to the savanna.

She circled around the group at a distance to get upwind of them, wary of so many. They had crossed the Kwangani River and were already well into her hunting grounds. This was a crowd of humans, but also many other animals. Coyotes, dingoes, wallabies, kangaroos, snakes, and several others. And there was another smell with them—something sour and unnatural. It was nothing that Uraza could recall having encountered before, even with her thousands of years of memory.

She pulled up short as she peered over a small hillock to determine the best route of attack. She caught a slight movement out of the corner of her eye, but pretended not to notice. Instead, she looked over the hill and tensed, as if to charge forward. Then, with no warning, she leaped to the side.

The two figures hiding in the grass were caught by surprise, and Uraza effortlessly brushed aside the green cloak they were hiding under and pinned each of them with one of her front paws. They struggled instinctively, but she gave a low growl and they immediately stopped.

Under her left paw was a vervet monkey, looking up at her sheepishly with its pinched black face and gray fur. But the monkey didn't concern her. Nearly crushed under her right paw was a boy, still gripping a spear in his right hand. She leaned in close, sniffing him and staring into his eyes.

The boy and the monkey had been hiding under a green cloak the same color as the grasses of the savanna, and the boy was covered from head to toe in mud. Despite herself, Uraza smiled. The mud would have locked in his scent, allowing him to stalk the savanna unobserved, even by humans accompanied by spirit animals with a strong sense of smell.

"What are you doing here?" Uraza demanded quietly. "You wear the goatskin of the Vendani, and know how to hunt the grasslands. So you must know that it is forbidden to trespass on my hunting grounds."

The boy gulped nervously, but then looked her straight in the eyes. "Yes, I know the laws of the savanna. But they don't matter now. I'm here to save you."

Uraza rocked back on her haunches, shaking with laughter. "You're just a boy with a spear. Perhaps I'll spare you, since you're clearly insane. A Great Beast doesn't need a little kitten like you to help her."

But the boy looked back calmly. "I'm not a boy. I endured the Nights of Fire and summoned Omika, my spirit animal. I'm a man, a warrior. I'm Tembo of the Vendani — and I'm going to save you, Great Beast or not."

Uraza pulled her paws back, and the monkey jumped around the boy's neck, hissing at her. "Very well, little warrior. I know enough of the Vendani — the word means 'goat thief' in many languages. How is a goat thief possibly going to save a Great Beast?"

The boy bristled. He looked her in the eye. "The Conquerors below aren't here to hunt your game. They're here to hunt you. To capture you and to steal something from you."

Uraza growled, and the boy's monkey dove to hide behind his back. Tembo himself didn't flinch. "How do you know this?" she asked.

"One year ago, they offered my people a truce, but on the first night after the peace was made, they took us by surprise. They torched our village. They slaughtered our goats, every one of them."

The massive leopard knew what that must have meant to the boy's tribe. The Vendani were goat herders. They ate goat meat, goat milk, and goat cheese. They wore goatskins. Vast herds of goats were their pride, and their wealth. The Vendani were renowned throughout Nilo as fierce warriors who would defend their herds from thieves, jackals, and even lions.

"Most of us surrendered on that day. But I swore that my people would be free. I am part of a small resistance.

Three days ago, I snuck into the camp of the men below to steal their supplies. I overheard them bragging that they were coming into your territory to capture you. They hope to find something hidden in your hunting grounds."

Uraza stretched, flexing her muscles. "Human swords and bows are no threat to me."

Tembo shook his head. "They have some sort of weapon that they think will give them an advantage. Give me time to sneak in again and discover their secret, and then we'll beat them together."

Uraza simply laughed at him, sending his monkey scurrying for cover again. "They are arrogant fools. And you are just as much a fool for thinking I need you. Watch me drive them from my lands, and I'll let you go home to tell stories of the ferocity of the Great Cat of the Grasslands."

She expected him to continue begging her not to go, but the boy just gave her a long look, then shrugged. "If you want to fight alone, I won't stop you."

The cat reached out a paw and pinned him to the ground again, letting her claws come out just enough to press dangerously into Tembo's neck.

"I'm the greatest predator on the continent. Better even than that miserly fool, Cabaro. I don't need your help. I don't care for your kind, and I will have nothing to do with your petty conflicts."

Tembo just raised an eyebrow as the claw dug into his flesh. "Are you trying to convince me, or to convince yourself?"

Uraza pushed him away, sending the young warrior rolling into the tall grass. "Watch," she thundered, and leaped over the hill, then charged down the grass toward the invaders.

In the camp below, there were shouts of alarm. The huge leopard let out a roar that shook the grasslands. Her body flew, legs surging with ancient strength. She was fury in the flesh, and she smashed through the first Conquerors without slowing. She dove into a knot of them, sending humans and spirit animals flying. Swords barely nicked her fur, and arrows felt like tiny pinches. *Let that foolish kitten on the hill watch how a Great Beast protects her territory,* she thought.

The center of the camp was emptied in moments, with most Conquerors fleeing and those who stayed falling easily to her claws. The sour scent was stronger here, and as a woman with an ax charged her, she noticed that its edge was coated with a sticky black substance.

Poison? Uraza smiled, baring her fangs. That was their secret weapon? Humans had tried to poison Great Beasts before. Arsenic, hemlock extract, plagues — it didn't matter. They were the rulers of the wild, and they were immune to poison and sickness. She batted the ax away effortlessly with a paw, and sent the Conqueror reeling with a sweep of her tail.

There were shouts from the grasslands outside of the camp, where the Conquerors were re-forming. Uraza stalked out of the camp to meet them, slashing a few tents and leaving them collapsing behind her as she went.

The foreigners had formed a shield wall, a barrier of tall steel shields bristling with spears. Uraza advanced, and arrows flew from behind the wall. They mostly bounced harmlessly off of her, but occasionally one would dig into her hide. There was a tingle with each puncture, but the sensation was no worse than a slight prick.

She surged forward, trying to push their spears aside with her paws, but there were too many. Uraza leaped to the left, and the Conquerors pivoted in unison, spinning the wall to face her. She jumped back to her right, but they hustled to adjust, keeping the forest of spears pointed at her. She backed up slowly, growling.

Then she charged, paws thundering on the ground as she gained speed. The soldiers ahead of her dug in, lowering their spears and bracing against their shields. More arrows flew at her, buffeting her like a wind of thorns. She grinned, showing them the white of her fangs. She could see their eyes go wide, but the spears stayed pointed straight at her.

Just moments before she reached the spears, Uraza leaped. She launched into the air, sailing high over the shields. Only one of the enemies managed to raise his spear in time, and it raked along her side. She felt a burning as the black substance coating its blade rubbed into the wound.

The leopard landed among the archers, sending them sprawling. With a few slashes from her claws, more Conquerors fell before her. But something was wrong. She leaped backward and felt a strange weakness in her legs. More arrows thudded into her at close range, each bringing with it a burst of the burning sensation from the black substance.

Uraza backed away slowly, her muscles quivering feverishly. Something was sapping her strength, weakening her with every passing moment. Now the Conquerors advanced, forming a ring with their spears pointing in at her. This was how tribes like the Vendani hunted lions, not a Great Beast like her. This was an insult.

"I am Uraza, undisputed queen of the grasslands," she bellowed. "You will leave my lands, or I will kill every one of you."

The leader of the Conquerors motioned, and the circle tightened. She was a tall, imposing woman, with teeth sharpened into points that matched the serpentine crest on her helmet and the lizard curling around her neck. "Be a good kitty, and lie down nice and easy," she said.

Uraza roared and charged forward, but she was greeted by a cluster of spearpoints and was forced back. The poison-tipped weapons left several new wounds in her coat. She knew that a Great Beast's body would adapt to this substance, but it would take time. That wouldn't help her now. Her feline instincts told her that she didn't have the strength to defeat this many. She turned to run, but they had her surrounded.

As her vision became blurry, the circle tightened. She gave a feeble roar and attempted to charge for the weakest point in the ring, but her legs buckled. The enemy advanced, spears lowered and dripping with the black poison.

She lashed out, but the more weapons pierced her, the more the burning grew, coursing through her legs and making her shoulder muscles spasm. She fell down into the grass, and struggled to stand again. Her legs refused to respond. She could do nothing but snap her jaws at the humans.

The last thing she saw before a curtain of darkness

descended was the Conqueror woman's crocodile grin as she advanced.

⟿⟾

The floor shook unsteadily and was decorated with bars of light. Uraza drifted back to consciousness slowly as her body healed itself. She raised her head as her vision cleared, and saw the bars of a cage had cast the pattern on the floor. They were massive—each as thick as one of her forelegs.

She stretched and stood, barely able to extend to her full length in the confines of the cage. She pushed her head against the bars, testing their strength. The cage was held in a massive wagon, pulled by a team of a dozen oxen.

The Conqueror woman walked up alongside the wagon with her spirit animal, a foot-and-a-half-long tuatara lizard that wrapped around her neck. "Ah, the kitty is awake," she said cheerfully.

Uraza growled. "Who are you? Who would dare to hold a Great Beast against her will?"

The woman smiled, revealing her pointed teeth. "I'm Samilia, the woman who will be queen of Nilo. And I can't have any competition from you, can I?"

The impertinence of this woman was shocking. Did she not know who she was speaking to? Uraza threw herself against the bars with a snarl. The bars slammed back into her, sending her reeling. The wagon shook only slightly, and the bars were undamaged.

"Oh, don't bother. I had this cage built especially for a big, nasty kitty like you."

Uraza clawed at the door to the cage, but succeeded only in leaving tiny scratches in the metal and dulling her claws.

"You're my ticket to owning all of Nilo, you know," Samilia continued pleasantly, ignoring Uraza's increasingly frenzied attempts at escape. "I used to be the leader of a small band of brigands in Zhong. Now the Reptile King has given me an army large enough to conquer this land and pacify it. And all he asks in return is that I deliver your talisman to him. With you out of the way, I'm sure my troops will have no problem scouring your territory to find the little trinket."

Uraza raged, smashing herself against the bars again. "The people of Nilo will not accept this insult. They will not tolerate you capturing their Great Beast. I *am* Nilo."

The woman just laughed. "We've eaten their livestock, burned their villages, and stolen their crops. And in all that time, you did nothing to help them. They curse you as much as they curse me, if not more. Did you know, at first the prisoners we captured threatened that you would come to their aid?" She shook her head. "But you never did, you bad kitty. So we don't hear that much anymore."

Uraza glared at the woman.

"But you don't have to suffer. You don't have to be part of this war. Just tell me where your talisman is, and once I have it, I'll let you go. You see? There's no reason we can't be friends."

Uraza snarled at her and turned away.

"Very well. I'll just find it myself," Samilia said with a shrug, then turned to walk to the other end of the caravan.

The wagon rolled along a dusty road, past the wreck-age of war. The great cat watched through the bars as they passed encampments and lines of marching soldiers. As they caught sight of the caged leopard, many cheered. Uraza growled and hissed at them, but that only encour-aged them.

They rolled past fields, barren and unsown. Past vil-lages burned and destroyed. Past lines of prisoners, proud warriors who had been forced to surrender by the invad-ing army. She saw the colors of many tribes, universally tattered and weary. Some looked at her with disappoint-ment, some with despair, and some with contempt. Others simply looked past her, eyes dead and defeated.

That night, Uraza's wagon was parked at the edge of a large encampment. They offered her no food or water, not that she would have accepted it anyway. A group of Conquerors stood guard, led by a large bald man with an eye patch.

Slowly, the camp fell silent as the Conquerors finished their meals and went into their tents. The moon rose, flooding the savanna with blue light. Uraza threw back her head and roared her fury into the night.

Uraza tried to pace, nervous energy overcoming her. But there wasn't room even to move the length of her cage, and she had to make do with walking in circles. Her legs quivered impatiently. She should be running through the grasslands, hunting for her next meal. No leopard was meant to be caged, least of all a Great Beast.

It was well after midnight when Uraza turned around to hear shouts at the edge of her camp. Her eyes adjusted in the dark. A human would only have been able to make out vague shapes, but as Uraza's eyes focused, she took in the whole scene.

The Vendani boy she had met just before she was captured was charging across the camp. The Conquerors were drawing their swords, but he was moving too fast. Not quite the speed of a leopard, but close. He was charging straight for her, but what was he doing? Humans. She admired his bravery, but he had the dumb loyalty of a dog, not the cunning of a cat.

The large one-eyed man stepped in the way, drawing a nasty-looking scimitar. Tembo stopped, glancing at Uraza. She turned her nose up and looked away from him.

"Stupid boy. You can't defeat all of them," she called out as he faced off with the large man.

Tembo simply grinned at her and raised an eyebrow. Then he threw the spear. It sliced into the large man, who stumbled back. He must not have expected that the boy wearing the green cloak would give up his only weapon. The bald man screamed in pain and fell to the ground.

As the other guards charged, Tembo danced to the side and started running again, back away from camp. A group of the Conquerors charged after the boy. Uraza watched as he reached the top of a hill, pulling away from the pursuit.

Uraza scraped her claws against the bars of the cage in frustration. If this boy thought he could kill an army of Conquerors one by one, he was more of a fool than she thought. Even as his pursuers disappeared on foot into the distance, another group was saddling up horses.

A moment later they raced off into the night, urging their horses to go faster.

Uraza lay down in the cage. The Conqueror woman had been right about the Niloans not rising in her defense. And now there was nothing one foolhardy boy could do. Should she have done more to help them? Things had been simpler in the time before humans had spread to every corner of the continent.

The camp was in an uproar. The sound of the injured guard's shouts as another Conqueror removed the spearhead filled the air. Uraza watched out of the corner of her eye as a small shadow detached from one of the tents and dodged through the crowd, making its way to the injured guard. While the bald man screamed, the shadow grabbed something from its belt.

The shadowy figure then zigzagged its way between the legs of the Conqueror soldiers.

Uraza turned to look directly at it. It was the goat thief's monkey, Omika! The creature nimbly dodged past the men and jumped onto the wagon. In her teeth, she held a key ring.

Uraza stood, flexing her muscles. "Open it," she demanded. The monkey squeaked back in reply.

Unseen by the Conquerors, Omika slid the key into the lock, and the cage door swung open. The leopard jumped out of the cage, sending any unfortunate Conquerors who happened to be nearby flying. With a few swats of her paws, she dispatched those who tried to fight her. The rest fled, sprinting for the relative safety of the camp.

Uraza stretched, savoring her freedom. Their poison would be useless now. She would tear this camp apart, and show them the folly of angering a Great Beast.

But the monkey jumped in her way. Omika squealed and tossed a handful of grass at her, then pointed at the savanna.

Uraza growled at the shrill little demon. "The boy. You want me to help him?" He might outrun the Conquerors who had initially chased him, but he would surely be run to ground by the mounted ones who followed.

For a moment she considered simply swallowing the insolent monkey whole, but surprised herself by circling around and changing course. The boy had risked his life to help her escape. And the Conquerors chasing him deserved her wrath just as much as the ones in the camp.

She turned and loped into the grasslands. Uraza was hunting again.

When Uraza caught up to Tembo, he was at the end of a ravine, in the rocky outcroppings between the grasslands and the veldt. She crept to the edge of the top, looking down on the humans and animals below. He was cornered by a group of armed Conquerors and their animals, mostly dingoes, emus, and other animals from Stetriol.

Tembo had somehow gotten hold of a spear and was backed up against the wall as the Conquerors advanced.

"Just give up, boy, and we won't hurt you," one of the Conquerors was saying.

"I'm tempted to make you the same offer," Tembo answered. "But I don't have time or patience to escort a bunch of prisoners around. I guess I'll just have to kill you." He hefted the spear threateningly.

The Conqueror laughed. "Brave boy, thinks he's funny. Now he's going to be a dead boy."

The soldiers advanced, and Tembo fanned his spear in a wide arc, trying to hold them back. They pushed forward anyway. But as the first Conqueror swung at him, Uraza dropped to the floor of the ravine, laying the lead attacker out with one paw. The others drew back. The giant leopard roared, shaking the ravine with the sound.

"It's the cat!" one of them yelled.

"Run for it!" another answered.

Within seconds, the Conquerors were running out of the ravine, armor clanking as they slammed into each other in their haste to escape.

"Thanks for the help," Uraza growled to Tembo in a low voice, then turned to charge after the fleeing enemy.

"Don't chase them. We don't have time," Tembo said.

Uraza turned back to him. "We? You helped me. I just helped you. We're even."

Tembo grinned. "Really? I stole you from my rivals. By the laws of the Vendani, you belong to me now."

"I'm not one of your goats, boy," Uraza growled, advancing on him.

"If I had done nothing," Tembo continued, "I would be safely in the grass and you would be in a cage."

Uraza gave him a hard stare.

"Fine," Tembo said. "We can argue about how great a friend I am later. I was spying on the Conquerors all day, and I heard their plans. That woman with the filed teeth, Samilia, is leading a force into your hunting grounds. One of the elders told them where your talisman is hidden."

"None of you know that," Uraza answered, looking back out into the grasslands. "No human has ever laid eyes on my talisman."

Tembo shrugged. "So no one knows it's buried in the Red Orchard?"

Uraza turned back with a roar. "How do you know that?"

"Don't blame me," Tembo answered. "I just heard them talking. But we need to go now, in order to stop them. We have a better chance if we work together."

Uraza simply laughed. "Stay out of my way, little warrior," she rumbled, then leaped out of the ravine and disappeared into the night.

The giant leopard prowled under ancient red trees. She had been expecting to find soldiers, spirit animals, and tents—but the orchard was deserted. There was no prey here, but their signs and their musky scent were everywhere.

This had been her hunting ground since ancient times, and now it was desecrated. Trees were reduced to splintery stumps, chopped for firewood. Trenches had been dug for latrines, and the grasses were trampled by scores of boots.

Uraza raced through the orchard, heart beating faster with each step. When she reached the tallest tree, where her talisman was buried, she slowed. Someone was there.

She crept forward with the sort of grace that only a Great Cat could command. Then she stopped short.

Somehow, the pip-squeak boy had gotten there first. He stood underneath the branches of her favorite tree, staring at a hole in the ground.

"You!" she hissed. "How are you here?"

The little warrior gave her his obnoxious grin.

"A leopard, a gazelle, a zebra—you all run so fast. But you tire out. A Vendani warrior can run all day and all night, slow and steady. When we hunt, we chase until the prey just can't run any farther."

She advanced. "Where is the talisman?"

Tembo gestured at the hole in the ground. "If it was here, the Conquerors have it now. We'll have to track them down."

Uraza drew closer, her massive head dwarfing the boy's small frame. "It's my talisman, in my hunting grounds. Go fight your battles somewhere else, little warrior."

Tembo shook his head, seemingly unconcerned with the enormous jaws inches from his face. "Really? What's your plan, then? Defeat an entire battalion by yourself?"

"I am a hunter. They are prey," Uraza answered, her voice low and full of menace. "They will regret their theft."

"Great," Tembo answered. "And while you're doing that, I'll be retrieving your talisman, which will be packed away in an iron wagon behind three locks. I saw it come off the ship last week.

"Don't worry," he said as she bared her fangs. "I'll give it back to you immediately. I just need to make sure they don't keep it."

"And how do you expect to do that?"

The boy shrugged. "A goat thief who can pick the lock on a paddock or barn can steal an entire herd in a single night." He leaned in with a conspiratorial air. "Before the Devourer attacked, my family had the largest herd on the savanna."

Uraza stared out into the fading light of the evening, where a herd of water buffalo was lazily grazing. Was she really going to accept help from this little human? She sat back on her haunches and sighed.

"Very well. But if you betray me . . ."

"You'll snack on my entrails? I'll warn you, I might be a bit stringy," Tembo answered, nonchalantly leaning in to examine the row of fangs still bared in front of his face.

They tracked the wagon trail through the night and into the next day, Tembo jogging easily alongside the Great Beast's long strides. Omika perched on the spear warrior's shoulders, chattering her wordless encouragement. From the freshness of the tracks and scents, Uraza could tell that they were gaining.

Evening fell as they reached the top of a rise. They found the wagon in a hollow below, empty and abandoned. Tembo knelt as Omika leaped around, poking and prodding.

"They camped here last night," the boy said. "And they left the wagon behind to move faster. They must have gotten word that we were free and likely hunting them."

Uraza nodded as she sniffed the ground. "Then they split into four groups, each going a different direction." She left unspoken the real problem: Even if they separated and she somehow trusted Tembo, they still would have no guarantee of catching up to the talisman.

They examined the tracks in silence for several minutes, while Omika gleefully raided a bag of feed left behind in the wagon.

Tembo stood up, looking into the distance. "They brought the talisman this way."

Uraza looked at him disdainfully. "How could you possibly know that? Any of these two-legged thieves could be carrying it!"

Tembo clucked at her with a scolding air. "Don't be so hard on thieves. We're not all that bad."

Uraza just snarled irritably, violet eyes flashing.

"Their leader, that woman Samilia," Tembo said. "I'd bet that she would keep the talisman herself. She has a great lizard for a spirit animal—her men called it a *tuatara*—and this group has a set of lizard tracks next to it. It must be hers."

Tembo started off following the set of tracks, with Omika trailing along, jabbering at him in her monkey nonsense. Tembo looked at her and nodded, as if he could understand the monkey's noises. Humans might speak with words, but Uraza had often thought that the sounds that came out of their mouths were equally meaningless.

As they drew farther away, Uraza looked around the camp. Then, with a noncommittal grunt, she lowered her head and padded along after him.

That night they stopped, and Tembo collected branches and built a small fire.

Uraza sat on her haunches and watched him quizzically as he spun a stick in a pile of tinder.

"That will attract attention," Uraza said. "If whatever you're doing to the poor stick actually works at all."

Tembo nodded. "We're near the village of Dakami. There's an old man living there that I befriended after he caught me stealing a baby goat. He's an ally. He'll see my signal and call my friends."

Uraza issued a full-throated noise, something between a growl and a purr. Tembo cast a wary glance in her direction, then quickly looked back at his work. Despite his bluster, Uraza could tell that the little warrior was still nervous around her. As he should be.

She put her head down and watched as the fire caught. Tembo held his cloak over the small blaze, periodically pulling it back to send precisely timed bursts of smoke into the air.

"Why?" she finally asked, when he had stamped out the fire.

"Why what?" He lay down in the grass, nestling into his green cloak.

Uraza gave him a long look, violet eyes glittering in the light of the dying coals. "Why risk your life for my talisman? Why fight against the Conquerors, when there are so many of them, and there's just a few of you? From what I saw, it looks like you've already lost."

"It's true, most of my tribe surrendered months ago." Tembo's face was still, staring up into the starry sky. "The village elders negotiated a deal with them, in order to keep us out of the war. But when they came, they destroyed everything anyway. We watched them torch our buildings, slaughter our livestock. My mother had a favorite goat, Maggi, the one that always gave us the most milk, and the best-tasting cheese. That woman, Samilia—she killed it and ate it right in front of us."

Tembo fell silent for a moment, and Omika nuzzled up against him.

"They didn't just take our livestock, our wealth. They took our way of life. Our honor. The elders said we couldn't fight. That they were too strong. But that first night after we surrendered, I stole back Maggi's last wheel of cheese and gave it to my mother. And I realized there wasn't anything that special about these Conquerors. The next day, I decided to leave my village. I stole a green cloak from one of their officers, in order to blend in with the grasslands, and fled."

Uraza watched the boy, wondering at the arrogance that had led him to take on an entire army alone.

"I met in secret with young men and women I knew from other villages and nearby tribes. I heard the stories of what the Conquerors had done, and told them mine. Everywhere I went, I stole the invaders' supplies, sabotaged their wagons, and always made sure that someone got a glimpse of my cloak, or Omika, so that they would know that it hadn't been a local who was responsible. It was when they demanded that spirit animals stay in their dormant state that I started to gain allies."

Tembo's voice had been tense and angry, but now he swelled with pride. "One night last spring, we all left behind our tribe colors and allegiances and replaced them with green cloaks, so that we could move undetected across the savanna. Everywhere we go, we bring hope that all will be free one day, and knowledge that the power of these Conquerors is not absolute. And we will fight, and win — with or without our Great Beasts."

Tembo seemed to be waiting for her to respond, but Uraza let the pause stretch into a long silence, until finally she heard his breathing fall into the steady rhythm of sleep.

The next morning, Uraza loped along the savanna, Tembo jogging easily next to her. Omika, exhausted from the journey, had gone into the dormant state, disappearing into a tattoo on Tembo's arm. They passed hippos sunning themselves in the Kwangani River, and a flock of sandpipers flew overhead, heading to their breeding grounds for the season. Finally they reached an area where the acacia trees had all been cleared. For a mile, they passed only stumps and discarded branches.

They crested a rise, and Tembo motioned to stay down. They crept forward in the grass and hid behind a large stump. On an even taller hill ahead stood the Conquerors' camp. It was nearly a small city, and the center was surrounded by a wooden stockade. A central keep had also been constructed of wooden palisades. The tracks they were following led straight toward the camp.

Tembo pointed to a small red flag of a lizard under the black Conqueror banner. "That's Samilia's insignia. It means she's there right now and holding court."

The Great Beast's muscles tensed. "I will have her throat in my jaws."

Tembo shook his head. "There are too many of them. Our only chance is to get in and steal it."

Uraza glared at him. "Throat. Jaws."

The little warrior shrugged. "Well . . . I see your point. Perhaps we might be able to fit in a little side mission." He looked back the way they'd come. "Let's go meet the rest of the resistance. We'll need them to pull this off."

Uraza left reluctantly. She would rather have just charged in and hunted down that Conqueror woman, but

Tembo had a point. There was an army in there, and they were dug into their defenses.

That night they met the resistance fighters at the one tree still standing within miles of the enemy fort. It had been burned out by a lightning strike, and was a charred wreck not suitable for building. Several of the smaller ones cowered in the back, wide eyes never leaving her huge, muscled form. Uraza could smell the fear coming from them. Even the most fearsome of them, a man fully an arm taller than the rest, was gripping his ax so tightly it looked like the wood might splinter. He had the tattoos of the Takweso people running down his bare chest, intertwined with a Niloan wild dog tattoo—his spirit animal in a dormant state. From what Uraza knew of the local tribes, the Takweso were ancient rivals of Tembo's Vendani. But the massive man gave Tembo a crushing hug as he arrived.

"Djantak!" Tembo said as he embraced the man.

"Goat thief!" Djantak answered with affection.

Tembo introduced Uraza to his fellow rebels: Djantak, the big Takweso man with the wild dog spirit animal; Kinwe, a bespectacled little man with an owl who peered down at them from the top of the tree; Jinta, a small, quiet girl with throwing knives and no apparent animal, and several others.

They were a ragged group, many of them a good deal younger than the usual age of Niloan warriors. And they all wore an assortment of green cloaks and capes, from rough cloth to what looked like a woman's decorative scarf wrapped around a little boy.

These human children should have been playing in the streets of villages and helping herd goats and sheep to watering holes, not fighting a desperate resistance for their freedom. How could their village elders have surrendered and left this mess for them to fix?

And yet that was the way of the wild. Often the young matured fast or not at all. This was not Uraza's concern. She hadn't created this situation. "Why do we need so many to sneak in and steal my talisman?" Uraza asked.

"Steal your talisman?" Tembo grinned.

"You're a madman, goat thief," Djantak muttered.

"We're going to do much better than that," Tembo continued. "We're going to burn that place to the ground, and their supplies and weapons along with it."

Djantak pulled back his cloak, revealing a cluster of waterskins. "Lamp oil, saltpeter, and birthwort extract. Liberated from a captured Zhongese caravan," he said. "These could make a blaze from a heated insult."

Jinta gave a menacing grin and held up a chunk of flint. She struck it with one of her daggers, creating a small shower of sparks.

"I'm here for my *talisman*," Uraza growled. Loudly. "Not a supply raid." All the resistance members save Tembo backed away from her nervously, their eyes wide. Djantak raised his ax defensively, then slowly lowered it to his side.

Tembo nodded. "I'm going after your talisman myself. The fire will be the perfect diversion."

The leopard cocked her head at him. "And what is my role supposed to be in all this, little warrior?"

Tembo gave his infuriating grin. "I'm going to ride you in, and then jump from your back to the top of the tower wall. Over a short distance you're much, much faster than I am—we'll be in before they can even close the gate."

Uraza leveled a stare at him, a look that had frozen whole herds of wildebeests in terror. "No human is going to ride me. You need a new plan."

The two locked gazes for a second, but Uraza was unyielding. If this boy thought he could ride a Great Beast, he was going to find a claw through his throat. "I am the mightiest predator in Nilo, boy. I'm not your beast of burden."

Tembo looked at her for a long moment, but she stared back with complete resolve. He nodded. "All right. We'll just have to be stealthy, and hope we can get close before they raise the alarm."

They struck out just before dawn. During the night, Jinta had used the cover of darkness to sneak up to the camp's palisade and weaken the stakes in a large section. Uraza crept forward, slinking through the grass alongside the green-cloaked humans. Though many times their size, the Great Leopard was a more than able stalker. When she did not wish to be noticed, eyes simply moved past her. They reached the palisade, and she waited while Tembo and Djantak quietly dislodged the wooden slats. How had she ended up here, reliant on humans to do things for her? She'd developed a certain fondness for her little warrior, but now a whole crowd of the smelly things surrounded her.

Tembo motioned for silence. They huddled down as a pair of guards passed by on the wall above them. The conversation drifted down in the early morning air.

"She's pushing us hard," one of the Conquerors was saying. "The troops are exhausted."

"But she got the talisman," the other answered. "The last few tribes in the south are surrendering, and northern Nilo won't be far behind. She'll probably go after the lion, Cabaro's, next."

Uraza could almost hear the evil grin as the first man spoke. "I can't wait to burn some of those villages, once they surrender. The look on their faces is just priceless."

"And then we can finally leave this ugly mudhole behind," the other answered. Their bootsteps began to recede.

Uraza started to growl, and Tembo put his hand on her flank to quiet her. She glared at him, but grew still.

Once the hole was cleared, they each wriggled through and crept from building to building on the other side of the stockade. It was still and calm inside, almost unnaturally peaceful. The rest of Tembo's warriors spread out and disappeared into the early morning grayness as Tembo, Djantak, and Uraza made their way to the central building.

Djantak peered around the edge of one of the nearby makeshift wooden shelters.

"Guards, little brother. Many guards," he said to Tembo. "We'll have to go in from behind."

They skulked through the outlying huts, making their way to the rear of the main building. It was only a small two-story thing, with rough stockade walls and a shingled roof.

Djantak squatted and Tembo stood on his shoulders, bracing himself against the wall. With a low grunt, Djantak pushed up and Tembo grasped the top of the wall. He pulled himself up to be even with the roof and scrambled onto the shingles.

Once Tembo was safely in, Djantak disappeared into the morning fog.

Uraza backed up, took a few steps, and leaped to the top of the building. She soared through the air, a sleek arrow of predatory instinct. Another beast of her size might have made a crash, but she landed as delicately as a sparrow alighting on a branch.

There was a trapdoor in the roof, which Tembo easily slipped through, but Uraza had to wriggle and push her way in.

The room was bare. Not merely plainly decorated, but completely empty. There were even marks in the floorboards where furniture had stood, but it was now all gone. Tembo crept to the stairs but looked back, shaking his head.

"Nothing there," he whispered. "It's been stripped clean."

Uraza glanced around the empty room, her body tensing. "Samilia knew we were coming. This is a trap."

As she said it, a bell pealed outside. Tembo ran to the trapdoor and poked his head through it. "They're pouring out of the buildings," he yelled down. "Fully armed and armored."

Uraza flexed her muscles and bared her fangs. "You don't trap a Great Beast twice. I will destroy them all."

Tembo laughed. "I like the enthusiasm, but maybe we could try something with a higher chance for *my* survival?"

Uraza glared at him.

"Samilia has the talisman around her neck. I have a plan. I just hope they haven't caught the rest of our people yet." Tembo rubbed his arm absently. "As soon as I have the talisman, jump down and show them your claws."

Uraza said nothing. If he failed, she could still try a more direct approach.

Samilia's voice rang through the building. "Come on, kitty, I don't suppose you'd make this easy? Just surrender and this will all be over. I won't even kill your little goat thief friend."

A smile lit up Tembo's face. "No mention of the others. This should work."

"Very well, little warrior. I'll give you a chance. But if this fails, you're on your own."

Tembo shrugged, gripped his spear, and headed for the door while the leopard returned to the roof to peer down at the enemy.

Tembo was right—they had been prepared for this. A horde of Conquerors was surrounding the building, their armor giving off a dull gleam in the gray light.

"Hold on, I'm coming out!" Tembo's shout came from below.

A moment later, he was facing off with Samilia in front of the building. He looked tiny, standing there with nothing but his spear and green cloak, faced with a wall of swords, shields, and spears. Samilia stepped forward, her smile showing off her unnaturally sharpened teeth. Her lizard curled around her neck, mimicking her reptilian smile.

"Finally ready to surrender, goat thief? I think you'll find my dungeon quite comfortable."

Tembo shrugged casually. "Maybe. Do you have coconuts for Omika there? She likes a cup of coconut juice in the morning and the rest of the fruit for lunch."

Samilia's expression darkened. "Drop your spear and surrender, boy, or I'll take it from your lifeless body." The leopard's sharp violet eyes could see her own talisman dangling on a strip of leather around Samilia's neck, the Amber Leopard practically glowing in the predawn light. The idea that this awful human shared in Uraza's power by wearing the talisman sent a fresh wave of fury through her. Samilia gripped her sword, which would swing with vicious speed, her movements aided by the hunter's instinct that Uraza's talisman conveyed.

Tembo stuck two fingers to his lips and let out a whistle that pierced the morning air. Then two things happened at once.

First, the stockade shook with the sound of explosions. In four places around the camp, fires suddenly sprouted into the air. Conquerors spun around in confusion, pointing at plumes of smoke at the edges of the stockade.

At the same time, Tembo stuck out his arm. A streak of energy came off of his wrist, and in a burst of light, Omika appeared – right on Samilia's shoulder. It happened in a blink, too fast even for Samilia's talisman-hastened speed. Before the woman could think to react, Omika grabbed the talisman and ripped it from her neck. Uraza was stunned – the ability to control exactly where a spirit animal appeared was not something that she had ever heard of. The two must have spent a long time practicing, to learn this trick.

Omika jumped toward Tembo just as Samilia swung at the monkey with her jagged sword. The woman's arm was fast, but no longer quickened by the power of the talisman. Omika lengthened and burst into light as she moved, and by the time the blade reached the monkey, she was nothing but a streak of energy. Tembo caught the talisman in his left hand while Omika appeared as a tattoo in the dormant state on his right wrist. Tembo raised the talisman in his hand, and Uraza leaped down.

The leopard roared with joy, finally able to strike at the enemy after so many days of pursuit. They had been distracted by the explosions, their neat lines shattered. She easily charged through them as discipline evaporated.

Conquerors went flying, struck by a whirlwind of claws and fangs. For a long minute she let the rage consume her as she pressed her revenge on the mass of enemy soldiers. Uraza purred gleefully as she saw Samilia retreating, guarded by shield-bearing Conqueror soldiers.

It was only when the enemy fell back to re-form that Uraza realized she had lost track of Tembo. She followed his scent through the smoke and found him lying on the far side of the camp, an arrow protruding from his right leg. He had a firm grip on the talisman, but wounded as he was, both were easy targets for the enemy.

The scene was now cast in an orange glow as towering flames lit up the stockade. Buildings in the interior were starting to catch as well, straw roofs going up in smoke first.

Some Conquerors were running, but Samilia had pulled together a large contingent and was forming a shield wall with them. In the firelight, her sharpened teeth gleamed as she ordered her soldiers to prepare themselves. She caught Uraza's eye, and in her gaze was something that surprised the Great Leopard: triumph.

That was when she noticed the lizard. It moved like water, slithering over and past the injured Tembo, carrying away the Amber Leopard talisman as easily as a river abducts a leaf.

Uraza yowled, a sound that shook the whole camp, and lunged for the tuatara. But it was too fast, was already halfway up Samilia's leg by the time Uraza had reached Tembo.

"There are too many," Tembo said, gasping for breath. "And I can barely move. Get your talisman back and run. You can still stop her."

The enemy closed in, a curtain of steel. Behind the line, Samilia cackled in victory. Uraza weighed the odds. Could she defeat them? Her sinews tensed, ready to charge in. One good blow could scatter them and break the wall. She had reserves of strength untapped, and the body of a Great Beast was an incredibly resilient thing. Uraza glanced at the brave little goat thief, trying to push himself up with one hand, his spear at the ready in the other.

She might win her talisman back, but he was already hurt, and would almost certainly not survive.

"No, little warrior," she said. "You're going to live to continue this fight." She lowered onto her haunches. "Climb on."

Tembo didn't wait for her to ask twice, almost jumping onto her back despite his injured leg.

"Hold tight," Uraza commanded. "And if you tell anyone about this, I'll eat you and your monkey both."

She could feel Tembo gripping tightly to her fur. As the shield wall charged, Uraza lunged forward. She crashed through the end of their line, then accelerated down one of the streets. The flames had overtaken most of the stockade wall, including the gate. The heat of the dry season had left this fortification as kindling, ready to burn with the slightest provocation.

She dodged past falling timbers from one building and a Conqueror charging from another. They arrived at the hole that they'd entered through, but it was blocked by fallen logs and smoke.

They were both starting to cough as smoke began to choke the air.

"We need another way out," Tembo croaked.

"Don't let go," Uraza answered, picking up even more speed as she raced across the ground. Finally, with a burst of strength, she leaped into the air. She could feel Tembo clinging tightly to her back as she barely cleared the bottom of the flames, leaving the fur on her feet singed.

Uraza loped across the savanna, leaving the burning stockade to light up the horizon behind her.

⌘

They met the others at the lightning tree, where Jinta removed the arrowhead from Tembo's leg while Djantak and the others held him down. A knife heated by flame cleaned his wound. Afterward, the humans sat around the fire, retelling stories of the raid and the various mishaps and near-disasters that had occurred. Though he claimed he would have survived anyway, to hear the others tell it, Djantak had only escaped because a log had fallen on a group of enemies who had him cornered.

Uraza sat out of the ring of firelight, staring into the savanna night. She had lost her talisman. For the humans this was a celebration, but for her, it was as if a part of herself had been torn away in the battle. She watched the moon drift up from the horizon.

The Conquerors would keep coming. She was sure of that. Though they had what they had come for, this "Reptile King" would not stop until the whole continent was under his thumb. The whole world, perhaps. She had seen the marching lines of them while in the cage. There were just too many. Even a Great Beast couldn't kill them all by herself.

"Djantak says I'll be back in working order in a few weeks or so," Tembo said, using a crutch to limp out of the firelight and stand next to the leopard.

"That is good," Uraza answered.

They both remained silent for several minutes, watching a flock of black herons winging across the night sky, on their way to feed in the salt flats of the Kwangani River delta.

"Thank you," Tembo finally said. "I don't know why you did it, but you did. All I can give you now is my gratitude, and the promise that we'll keep searching for it. Keep fighting."

Uraza lowered her eyes. Human promises. From this one, maybe that meant something.

"We got a message from our allies in Eura," he continued. When Uraza cast a curious glance in his direction, he nodded somberly. "People say the young King Feliandor of Stetriol has gone mad, and that he's aided by Great Beasts as well. These Conquerors aren't just in Nilo. They're moving across all of Erdas—and we must fight back wherever we can. There's a shipment of Conqueror siege weapons coming into Port Tantego next week. If we stop it, the city of Kalindi may be able to hold out through the wet season."

"Then you'll be headed there, I suppose," Uraza said, looking away from Tembo once more. Though she did not show it in front of the human, the news that some of her fellows were helping these plunderers deeply troubled her. She had not felt the presence of her neighbor Kovo recently.

"*We're* headed there, you mean," Tembo answered. "I stole you, so you belong to me. We've been over this."

"I should just eat you now, you insolent boy," she rumbled.

Tembo shrugged. "What makes you think you could take me in a fight?"

Uraza placed a massive paw on the boy's chest, letting it sit there so that he could feel its weight. But Tembo just grinned back at her.

"You're nothing but a handful of kittens," Uraza said, sprawling out to sleep. "Without me, you'll get yourselves killed for sure. I don't think I can give Samilia that satisfaction."

Tembo smiled as he reached over and scratched the leopard behind the ears. Uraza's claws extended reflexively, but she had to admit, it felt good. She should put a claw through his throat for presuming to do this. But somehow she found herself purring.

He had helped her out of a difficult trap. He had been willing to sacrifice his own life for her Amber Leopard, even when she had turned a blind eye to his people. She could tolerate his impertinence, she supposed. Just this one time.

Briggan

THE PACKLEADER

By Emily Seife

Leaping over a fallen log, Katalin cursed herself again for the carelessness that had landed her in this position. She had been running for almost half an hour, ever since she'd stupidly stumbled right into a Conqueror's camp, attracting his attention.

The Conqueror was big and strong, but she was faster, and she'd been sprinting hard. Was it possible that she'd managed to escape him? She glanced behind her. She couldn't see far through the pouring rain, but she seemed to have lost her pursuer for a moment. If so, there was no point in continuing to stumble through the woods, possibly attracting his attention as she crashed through slippery bramble. Spotting a rocky crag, Katalin ducked underneath it and crouched toward the back of the stone overhang. A moment later, she saw a wave of shadow slip through the rain and then appear beside her.

Shaking the rain out of her eyes, she smiled at the dark form as it rippled up her leg and perched on her shoulder. It was Tero, a sleek black mink and her spirit animal. They had bonded only a year ago, but already she couldn't imagine life without her quick, sly companion. She nuzzled her cheek into his tiny body, allowing his thick fur to briefly warm the tip of her frozen nose.

Looking down, Katalin realized that her tattered cloak was so dark with rain that it appeared as black as Tero's own fur coat, not the true pine green that she knew it was. If anyone came upon her now, they would never recognize her as one of the resistance. But she was – not just a member of the resistance of Marked people and their spirit animals against the Conquerors and their Reptile King – but one on an important mission that could be crucial to Eura's future. Adelle, one of the leaders of the resistance, had trusted Katalin with this. She had pressed the map into Katalin's hand, looking hard into her eyes, and told her that she had to find Briggan the Wolf, one of the fifteen Great Beasts, and convince him to join their cause.

They needed Briggan if they were to have any chance at all of winning the war. While the resistance was still scattered and untrained, the Conquerors were already organized and battle-hardened. They were led by the Reptile King – no, Katalin reminded herself, they did not use Feliandor's self-proclaimed title. The resistance called him what he truly was: *the Devourer*. For he and his army devoured land and lives. The Devourer was coldly calculating and controlling. Plus, his Conquerors were aided by two of the Great Beasts, the ape and the serpent. When impressing on Katalin the importance of her mission, Adelle had told her that their small movement would stand no chance unless they could get Great Beasts to join them.

Katalin made herself comfortable on the packed dirt, glad for the moment to rest and gather her thoughts. Tero, on the other hand, could never hold still except when sleeping. Getting bored, he leaped off of her shoulder and somersaulted across the dirt, pausing to snap at invisible bugs and to preen his beautiful coat. Katalin loved watching him move and play. He was always hungry, even when they weren't traveling across hard terrain all day, and he spent every moment of free time hunting. She'd seen him kill everything from flickering little fish to large birds.

When they had first bonded, her hands were always covered in cuts. Tero loved to nibble and used to bite her fingertips whenever she pointed or gestured. She was lucky to have been with the other Marked at that point. They had shown her how to enhance her bond with him, and ways to get him to respect and listen to her. Still, it had taken months until Tero was able to control himself, and even now he would sometimes give a reflexive little snap when she reached out to him. She thought she could read him well enough to recognize a slightly ashamed look that always followed after he forgot himself like that.

Shivering, she closed her eyes. Katalin had nightmares and could rarely get through a full night's sleep, but she'd learned to steal small catnaps, collecting snippets of rest. She was getting close to Briggan, and would need to gather her strength in order to face the Great Wolf. She felt confident that she could find him, even though the Great Beasts were known to be reclusive. She had the map from Adelle, of course. And using her bond with Tero, she could draw upon his hunting skills and become a skilled tracker.

It was what would happen when she found Briggan that she was worried about.

If anyone could turn their ragtag group of rebels into an army of green-cloaked fighters, it was he. Known as the Packleader, Briggan was a Great Beast, physically huge and extremely powerful, but like any regular wolf, he had a strong pack sensibility and never traveled alone. Rumor had it that wherever Briggan went, he was followed by the Great Pack, a large cabal of ferocious and fiercely loyal canines. The resistance hoped that Briggan would use that same powerful leadership to gather and inspire their disparate members.

Adelle had told Katalin all this before she sent her out on the mission. "You'll find Briggan in the Granite Hills," she'd said. "You'll recognize him when you see him, believe me." Katalin had nodded—everyone knew that the Great Beasts were enormous, and Briggan was known to have hypnotic cobalt-blue eyes. "He has a powerful presence," Adelle had continued. "So you'll need to be respectful, but able to hold your own. It's that very dominance that makes us need him to join us so badly. If he can use his leadership to guide our resistance and compel others to join us, it could change the tide of the war."

Change the tide of the war . . . Katalin liked the sound of that, and liked knowing that she could play a role in making it happen.

Still, though Katalin hoped Adelle was right, that the huge wolf would be an ally, he was also a dangerous wild animal, and so was his Great Pack. She wanted to be alert when they came face-to-face for the first time.

Katalin felt a silky touch on her cheek and smiled, thinking it was the tip of Tero's tail. No matter how much he cavorted, and how far he went on his little hunts, he returned back to her frequently to check in, letting her know he was still there.

Then she felt a sharp piercing sensation on her neck and she sprang up with a shriek, nearly banging her head on the low stone ceiling.

Two tiny glints of light shone from the rock overhang. As Katalin peered closer to make out the thing that bit her, a flurry of wings came at her and beat at her face. Katalin squeezed her eyes shut, but not before she saw that it was a tiny bat – a vampire bat – and it had a distinctly malevolent look in its beady eyes. Again it lunged at the exposed skin on her neck. She pushed it off with a flick of her arm, but it flapped its wings and quickly swooped up and out of her reach. She could feel small drops of blood moving down her neck, running in rivulets with the rain.

Katalin crouched down on the dirt floor. She tried to keep one eye on the bat as she scanned the rainy woods. It was possible that this was just a confused creature, but why would a nocturnal bat be out during the day? It seemed more likely that it was the spirit animal of the Conqueror who had been pursuing her.

Just then, the bat dove in again, tangling its webbed wings and feet up in Katalin's long hair, and beating at her eyes to disorient her.

With a rush, Tero leaped toward her and landed on her knee. Using it as a springboard, he bounced up onto the top of her head immediately. He swiped at the bat, snapping and clawing furiously. Katalin tried to stay calm, but with a battle being waged in her hair, it was hard to keep from crying out.

But if this bat was the spirit animal of her pursuer, as she thought it was, it was too late for caution – they had already been found.

Then there was a yank – followed by a thud – and Tero landed on the ground with the bat and a chunk of Katalin's hair pinned to the earth beneath him.

"Thanks, Tero," she said, rubbing the sore spot on her scalp where the hair had been pulled out in the scuffle. "I think."

He looked up at her, eyes glittering with mischief. She knew Tero was clever, that he had excellent instincts and a deep intelligence – but she wasn't sure he truly understood the seriousness of their situation. Caution didn't seem to be in his nature. He fed off of risk, and sometimes she could feel herself getting pulled into that dangerous current with him.

"We have to get out of here," she said sternly. "Now." She selected a large rock and carefully laid it down on the bat's wing so that it was pinned and immobilized, but not injured. It might be a Conqueror's spirit animal, but even so, she couldn't bring herself to kill it.

Katalin and Tero took off together. She could feel Tero's nimbleness infusing her body, making it easier for her to jump over rocks and tumble under low-hanging branches. Just as she started to think they'd left the danger behind again, a body came crashing through the leaves ahead, and a man landed right in front of them.

He was crouched in a fighting pose, holding a crude club. His dark, bushy eyebrows flared on his brow like two bat wings. Katalin could see the tattoo on his forearm — so he'd retrieved his bat and put the creature into its passive form.

"Hello there, little one," the man grumbled. "I've been trying to catch up with you for quite some time now. And on a rainy day like this one, I'd much rather be back at the camp in front of the fire."

Katalin shrugged. "The Devourer is lucky to have a soldier as hardy as you."

The Conqueror swung his club at her head. She reacted quickly, dropping to the ground just in time. Unable to stop the momentum of his swing, the club went crashing into a tree trunk, and it bounced out of his hand. "Mako! Come quick, I found the girl!" he shouted as he scrambled to recover it.

Katalin didn't wait to hear more. She took off at a sprint. A blind panic pushed her forward, her fear bringing back old memories . . . mixing them together with the present, so that she could hardly tell where she was. Her heart pounded so loudly she could barely hear anything else. Then Tero bounded up onto her shoulder, and she could feel his cool confidence surging through her, bringing her . . . not calm, but exhilaration. With that, she was able to start paying attention to her surroundings again, to hear with clarity the sounds of the forest: the thudding footsteps behind her, the rain and the wind in the trees — and then another sound, also a wet sound, but heavier. They were near a river.

She glanced at Tero, and his smiling eyes confirmed her instinct.

Swerving to the right, she followed the sound of the river. She picked her way through bushes and brambles, trying to keep her footing in the mud. Then the ground slanted steeply down, and Katalin lost her footing. She skidded down the bank to where the dirt gave way to a stone overhang. The edge of the bank came into view, revealing the water below. She couldn't stop herself, so she dropped down to hands and knees, throwing her body heavily at the earth and coming to a stop just inches from the precipice.

Her knees were scratched and muddy, but at least she hadn't gone careening off the edge. She had a moment to look around and figure out the best way to execute her plan.

All the heavy rain had swollen the river, making it deep and fast. That had its benefits if they decided to jump in and try to swim it – they probably wouldn't land on a rock, or hit their heads on the bottom – but on the other hand, there could be dangerous currents just waiting to drag her under with invisible hands. Still, both Katalin and Tero were excellent swimmers. It was a risk she was willing to take, especially when the danger behind them was even more certain.

Taking a deep breath, Katalin dove into the water, Tero right behind her. The water grabbed them, shockingly cold, and threw them downstream. The river tumbled them over and over, like dice in a cupped palm.

Back on shore, the leaves shivered and shook. The wet forest closed around the spot where they'd disappeared, holding their secret, as the Conquerors thundered by.

Katalin woke up with a start.

They had passed a deeply unpleasant night. The river had allowed them to disappear and lose the Conquerors, but when they crawled out onto a muddy bank a mile downstream, Katalin and all of her possessions were soaked through. Tero's coat dried quickly, but she spent a miserable night shivering and wet. When the rain stopped in the early hours of the morning, she had finally dropped off to sleep for a little bit. It was a restless sleep, veined with dark dreams.

No matter how hard she tried to lock up her memories, her mind kept circling back to the past, like a prowling animal. In her dream she had been back in her home village.

Her home had been in eastern Eura, the part closest to Zhong. The part closest to the Conquerors. When the Conquerors first swarmed out of Stetriol to begin their invasion, they started by swallowing the continents of Zhong and Nilo. They set their sights on Eura next. They'd started testing the waters, sending advance parties in on raids, to see what the resistance in Eura would be. They knew they wouldn't have the element of surprise that had allowed them to take mighty Zhong, but they suspected that Eura didn't have the organization or the power to resist.

And so Katalin had been harvesting crops with her family when the smell of smoke came creeping over the fields. They'd assumed that someone had been careless — brought a candle into a barn, left a hearth fire going without supervision. . . . All the workers had gone sprinting back into town to help. Fire was a terror, but one they knew. But when they reached town, armed only with buckets, there was more than fire. Wreathed in the smoke were men with swords, men whose mission was to slash and burn and reduce the town to nothing but a charred scar on the earth.

Her dream usually ended there, the shock of discovery shaking her awake. But last night the moment had been prolonged, haunted by howls of despair, full-throated cries of mourning. She thought she'd heard her father's voice, open and bare in a sound she had never heard from him before that day—

But something had awakened her. Had it been something real or imagined? A sound from the physical world or a cry from her nightmares? She crouched warily, squinting into the morning sunlight. Had the Conquerors found her again? But there was none of the hush that came when someone had startled the birds away, and her gut told her that they were not nearby. She relaxed and leaned back onto her bedroll, smoothing her sleep-rumpled hair back into a tight braid.

Her dreams were getting stronger. She'd been having these nightmares ever since her town was destroyed, but now the dreams were becoming more vivid, more realistic, the closer she got to Briggan. Adelle had told her that all the Great Beasts had special powers, and that Briggan—as well as being a pack leader—was often able to help enhance the senses. People even claimed that Briggan could bring visions. Glimpses of the future.

Well, that's not what she was getting, Katalin thought crankily. She'd welcome some vision of the future, some hint of what to expect. But she was being pushed further into her past.

Trying to shake off the lingering feelings from the dream, she looked around, getting her bearings. Her map was soggy, but she'd basically memorized it anyway. The river had deposited her at the base of a small foothill. Beyond that to the north was a flat plain, and then the Granite Hills where Briggan and his pack were believed to make their home.

Katalin decided there was no reason to delay any longer. Right now the Conquerers thought she was just a confused Marked girl who had stupidly stumbled into their path. They wanted to hunt her down, but wouldn't spend long dwelling on her now that she'd lost them. But if they caught on to her mission – to the fact that she'd been sent to find Briggan – they would never let her survive. With Tero as a curled tattoo on her arm, she started hiking north, her boots squelching.

Lost in her thoughts, the time passed quickly. At midday Katalin paused. She had made it over the heavily wooded hill and now her feet were sore. With the sun high and hot in the sky, it seemed like a good time to set up camp and allow her things to finish drying out. She could eat and rest, then she could keep moving again later under the cover of dusk.

She found a small, sunny clearing with room to pitch her tent. Tero sprang from her arm as she bent over to hammer the pegs into the soft earth. She gave him a stern glare that she knew would be lost on him.

"Oh, it's just like you to go passive when there are miles of tough terrain to hike, and to jump out right in time for some playing around." Tero twined his sleek body around her ankles apologetically. "Yeah, right. I'm sure you feel real bad."

There was a scampering noise in the trees, and a second later Tero was gone, a dark blur in the dappled shade, darting after whatever squirrel or bird had caught his attention.

"Thanks a lot!" Katalin called after him. "Great teamwork!" Sometimes it did bother her that her spirit animal was so fiercely independent.

She finished pitching the tent, then slung the waterproof food bag over a tree branch and hauled it up out of reach of any interested animals. She spread her clothing and other supplies out to dry. All that done, she pulled a twist of beef jerky out of her pocket and sat happily chewing on it, enjoying the sunshine and listening to the sounds of the forest around her. She could almost believe that the rest of the mission would be smooth sailing from here.

A moment before she heard it, she felt it, like a cold trail of ice water down her spine. Then the sound opened up and enveloped the sky. It was a lonely howl, one blast that froze her blood and sent goose bumps prickling across her skin. There was a long pause, and then the call was answered once, twice, three times. The hills rang with the sound of the wolf cries.

Immediately, Tero was beside her again, the fur on his back standing up in alarm. Katalin's heart melted at the sight of the tiny mink ready to take on a pack of wolves.

This must be the Great Pack. They were powerful and potentially dangerous, but there was no way to avoid them, not when her aim was to go even deeper into the heart of their territory, to Briggan.

The howls were clearly warnings, though – aimed right at Katalin. *Stay away*, they said. *Turn back*.

Briggan knew she was here.

After resting, Katalin packed her bag and continued her journey. Her path took her meandering downhill for a few hours. As she walked, the sun began setting in the west, lighting up the trees with an orange glow. It was beautiful, but the light reminded Katalin of the flames in her town. . . . She snapped her head back to the present. The valley was opening up below her. This was Briggan's valley. The land was ruled by a wolf – *the* wolf – and his Great Pack. Based on the howls she was now hearing frequently, the wolves roamed freely over this valley and the Granite Hills above.

She could see that the closest part of the valley was already in the shadow of the hill, but the far edge was still shining in the sun. Colorful jays darted around, snatching berries and singingly joyfully.

Then she caught sight of something – a small hut.

Katalin hadn't known that anyone lived out here in the northern woods. There were certainly no large cities, not even any towns that she knew of. But she supposed she shouldn't be too surprised that there would be people scattered around, maybe a farmer or a shepherd who liked the solitude.

It felt like it had been forever since she'd talked to

another person. Being attacked by a Conqueror didn't seem like it counted as real human interaction. She turned toward the house. She'd check it out, see if there was anyone there who could shelter her for the night, maybe even give her some tips on approaching Briggan. She'd have to be careful, of course. It was unlikely that someone living alone in Eura would be a friend to the Conquerors, so that didn't worry her. But there were many other forms that a foe could take.

Tero nipped at her shoe, clearly trying to tell her something. She watched as he scampered ahead, ran back, and scampered ahead again. He was watching her eagerly. He reminded her of an arrow strung taut on a bow, ready to speed off the second he was released. She knew exactly what he wanted.

"Okay," she said cautiously. "Go scout it out and let me know if it looks safe." He perked his head up. Before he could spring away she called, "But, Tero—take a look and then come right back. No fooling around." She gave him her sternest look, but the invisible leash had been severed—he was already shooting across the valley toward the hut.

Katalin crept slowly along the edge of the valley, closer but still out of sight. When she felt she was near enough, she sat down with her back against a tree to wait for Tero.

She waited . . . and waited. The sun disappeared behind the hills, and the entire valley was sunk into shadow. She squinted into the dusk, worried. He was supposed to get the lay of the land, then come fetch her or let her know to stay away. So where was he? Had he gotten into trouble? She pictured a maniac shoving Tero in a pot and making mink stew.

After waiting another few minutes, Katalin decided she had to go investigate, no matter what dangers might be in store.

She crept forward, trying to stay hidden in the shadows. The hut was just up ahead, and now she could see that there were a few chickens in a fenced-in yard outside. Tiptoeing even closer, she listened closely but couldn't make out anything besides the quiet clucks of the chickens.

Without Tero, she had trouble feeling the bold courage that she needed to face whoever lived here. She needed him to feed her with his playful curiosity and to warm her with his soft fur and little nudges. Otherwise, she felt very, very alone. Without her spirit animal, she felt like the girl she was before she'd received her mark, before she'd been welcomed into the resistance. A girl without a home, without a family—without anything except for a fear that took up so much of the space inside her that sometimes she forgot there was anything else.

But now Tero was probably somewhere in this house, maybe needing her, and so she had to summon her own courage, which may or may not exist, from someplace inside.

She gripped her small knife tightly in her fist and crawled over the hard-packed dirt yard to the window of the hut. Trying not to make a sound, she peered up over the windowsill.

In the warm light of the flickering fire, she saw someone bent over, pinning Tero to the ground.

In the second that it took her to jump up and shout "Hey!" in her most intimidating voice, she'd realized that the person was an old woman . . . and she was giving Tero a belly rub.

The mink was lying on his back, totally relaxed. His tongue lolled out of his mouth, while the old woman scratched his belly just the way he liked it. Katalin's first reaction was relief – her second, rage at her tiny betrayer.

Tero's bright eyes flicked up and caught sight of her. An apologetic look spread across his face. The old woman followed his gaze and smiled up at Katalin.

"You must be this little fellow's companion, hey? Well, come inside already." Katalin could hear the woman's voice through the glass pane. She reluctantly brushed the dirt off her knees, hauled her pack onto her shoulder, and walked around to the front of the house.

As she let herself in, the woman pushed creakily to her feet and welcomed Katalin with a warm embrace. She had short, curly gray hair and smelled like cinnamon. This was not the dangerous enemy Katalin had been anticipating.

"I'm Milena, welcome," she said. "Can I get you some soup? I don't have much food prepared – I don't eat all that much anymore – but I have some good soup here."

"No, thank you. I'm fine –" Katalin began, but the woman barely stopped to listen.

"Good, good. Let me get that soup heated up and then you'll have something filling to eat. Looks like you could use a real meal."

"I –"

"And this is your spirit animal, I take it? Don't worry, no need to be secretive with me. And anyway, I knew you were coming." She winked at Katalin.

Meanwhile, Tero was nudging her ankle impatiently, wanting to be forgiven. Katalin pushed him away with the side of her foot, not quite ready to give up her grudge. She'd been so frightened for him, and for no reason at all!

"You're looking for Briggan?" Milena asked suddenly. She stopped stirring the soup that she'd poured into a big pot, and looked carefully at Katalin.

"That's right. How did you know?"

"Yes, you're looking for the Great Wolf. Everything about you is seeking, seeking . . . " Milena popped a finger out of her mouth and licked her lips. "Soup's ready!"

She pushed Katalin into a chair and slid an enormous bowl in front of her. "You eat, I'll explain."

As Katalin spooned the fragrant liquid into her mouth, Tero slunk into her lap and curled up. She didn't acknowledge him — but she didn't push him off either.

"You might think I like to talk, but I run out of words quickly. It's just that I haven't seen anyone in a long while, so I have a lot stored up at the moment. I came out here to get away from people. . . . I like the quiet, like being on my own . . . but what I didn't expect was the power that Briggan would have on me. I'm sure you've heard that he can bring visions to those around him?"

Katalin didn't even try to respond, just nodded.

"Well, it's true. Probably more than the rumors would even suggest. Briggan can sharpen the senses. He can give people visions, or insight in their dreams. After I lived here for a while, I tried going back into the world. But I saw too much. It wasn't possible for me to walk around, pretending I couldn't see what was coming — it would be as though you tried to deny one of your own five senses.

People thought I was crazy too. The visions of the future that he brings are not fixed – they can be changed – but no one would listen to me, no one would let me help them. So I had to leave. Had to come back here."

The woman put her wrinkled hand on Katalin's arm. "I'm sure you've felt something in you change as you came closer to the Granite Hills. Don't be afraid. There's a reason that you're seeing whatever you're seeing. Even a peek into the past can be a vision of the future, waiting for you to sort it out."

Milena seemed to run out of words after that, caught up in something inside her own head. But she made a heaping pile of blankets so that Katalin and Tero could spend the night comfortably. Once they were snuggled together, the old woman stood over them and scattered some fragrant bunches of lavender over and around their bed.

"This will help soothe your sleep," she said. "One night's peace from the dreaming is all I can offer. After that, you'll have to sort through your memories, same as the rest of us."

Katalin couldn't remember ever having a better night's sleep.

The next morning, after their good-byes, Katalin and Tero left the hut and the valley behind and set off on another hard day's hike. This one was mostly uphill, taking them into the edge of the Granite Hills. The terrain grew tougher and the trees began to thin out.

While Adelle had not been able to tell Katalin exactly where Briggan would be, Milena had given her very specific directions. The Great Wolf made the highest hill his base, though there was no guarantee he would be there at any given time.

Milena had also handed the girl a small pouch, packed to the brim with sharp-smelling rosemary. "It's for the memory," the old woman had said, rubbing some of the leaves between her fingers to release the pungent smell.

Now Katalin headed uphill, hoping for the best, but after a whole day of walking, keeping her eyes peeled for giant paw prints, she hadn't spotted any sign of the Great Wolf. The wolf calls – both barks and howls now – were more frequent. They sounded closer than ever, though the animals kept themselves hidden from her.

That night, after making camp, Katalin opened the bag of rosemary and inhaled the fresh evergreen scent. She didn't quite understand what Milena had meant about memory, but the smell did remind her of happier times. Of meals cooked at home. She fell asleep early and slept deeply that night.

And she had another dream.

Katalin was with her best friend, Lizabeth. It was the Spring Festival, Katalin's favorite holiday. They were holding hands and running through the town, happily taking in all the excitement and decorations. Everywhere, giant blue flags with Briggan's symbol were flying, waving proudly in the wind.

It was local tradition to make strings of popcorn and dip them in sugar or chocolate or butter, and then hang them from the doorways. The treat symbolized birth, the emergence of something sweet from its hard winter shell.

And it was tasty too. All the town's children were out, jumping for the dangling strings.

Katalin and Lizabeth ran from doorway to doorway, snacking as they went, and sneaking looks through the windows into the homes, to see who had the biggest feast prepared. There were huge roast turkeys, trays of baked apples, bowls of fresh spring greens and edible flowers. . . .

When Katalin turned back to look at her friend, she saw that Lizabeth had managed to get chocolate all over her face, and Katalin burst into laughter.

But as they ran, the breeze grew from a light touch to something stronger, a howling wind. Katalin didn't notice at first—she was caught up with laughing and teasing her friend—but then Lizabeth pulled at Katalin's arm. Her eyes were big and afraid, and Katalin stopped abruptly. Suddenly all she could hear was the howling wind.

It tore down the flags and ripped the leaves off the trees. The howling grew and grew, swallowing the town—

Katalin snapped awake.

The dream had felt completely real.

The dreams always felt real. Each time, for a moment, she believed she was home. Then something came and tore it away from her, and she remembered who she was now: a girl with no home, no family, no best friend. Just a growling belly and an important mission. Katalin thought back to what Milena had said—that Briggan brought insight to dreams. That even a dream of the past could be a vision of the future. Great—did that mean that her future held as much destruction as her past?

She sat up and stuck her head outside her tent. And

took in the total destruction that had come to her camp-site while she slept.

Katalin gasped aloud. It had been utterly ran-sacked. The bags she'd left on the ground had been torn open, their contents scattered around the clearing in shreds. Her food bags, which she'd hung carefully from tree branches as always, were ripped open. Most of the food was gone, though she could see some scraps on the ground, covered in dirt. Animal prints wove through the destruction.

She glared down at her tattoo; of course Tero had been in his passive state just when she could have used his watchful eyes on her campsite.

It dawned on Katalin that she herself was unharmed. Her tent was untouched, and so was a circle of dirt about three feet in diameter all around it. There was something very deliberate about the damage – this was not just some hungry raccoon.

She leaped into a crouch and scanned the edges of the clearing.

There in the shadows, she could see the dark outline of an animal – a wolf. The creature's hackles were raised. It let out a low growl that sent vibrations through her bones.

"Hey!" she shouted, leaping toward it, not pausing to think about what she was doing.

Like a flash, it turned and bounded away through the woods.

It was gone, and so were all of her supplies.

The only thing left behind was the message. A clear warning from the wolves, and from Briggan himself. *Stay away.*

But that was not a message Katalin could afford to heed.

The farther they walked in the Granite Hills, the more frequent the howls and barks of the wolves became. Tero stayed close to Katalin now. He didn't show fear, but she could tell he was wary, uncomfortable. Of course his natural instinct would be to get away from this place filled with wolves.

One afternoon they were forging a path up a rocky hillside when Katalin heard a whining sound. She turned to see if Tero had heard it as well, and he was already frozen, ears perked. With his sharp hearing, he'd have heard it well before she did.

"Should we go check it out?" she whispered to Tero.

He darted along beside her as she made her way closer. It sounded like some kind of animal was in pain. Then she froze.

Voices. Human voices.

"He doesn't look that tough," a man's voice said.

"Not now, he doesn't," a woman answered. "But he will soon enough."

The animal let out a series of scared yips.

Katalin peered around the trunk of a thick tree. She could see a wolf caught in a trap. He didn't seem to be injured, just stuck.

Around him, at a safe distance, were two men and a woman. One of the men inched forward toward the wolf, then gave it a sharp kick. The wolf bared its teeth and tried to lunge at the man, but he quickly skipped back out of its reach. The movement only made the ropes that held the wolf tighten further. The animal yipped again, a mix of fright and outrage.

The wolves had been tormenting Katalin – scaring her and destroying her campsite – so that at times it felt like they were her enemies, instead of the pack of the Great Beast she was trying to convince to join their cause. But no matter how angry she felt at them, she never wanted *this*.

She could only make out small glimpses of the people between the trees, but one of them, the man who had just kicked the wolf, looked familiar. He glanced up, and she caught a better glimpse of him. Yes, it was definitely him – the Conqueror with the bat spirit animal that she'd escaped from a few days earlier. And now that she knew to look for it, she spotted his bat too, circling the sky above his head. She'd have to be very careful. The bat's keen hearing and higher perspective might give them away.

Katalin noticed another animal in the clearing – a fox. The animal was pacing back and forth in the grass. There was something about its face that looked unusual. It had the same alert look that many spirit animals had, but there was something darker in it too. She couldn't tell at first whether it belonged to the woman or the other man.

The man with the bat stepped forward, toward the trapped wolf. "He'll make a good spirit animal for you, Mako," he said to the second man. "The Bile will bind him to you, so that he'll have to do whatever you say. You'll be able to send him to the passive form at any time. And when he's not passive he'll be fierce. You can see it in his eyes."

Katalin couldn't make out anything in the wolf's white-ringed eyes except for a desperate fear. What was this Bile that the man mentioned?

The other man, Mako, looked slightly younger and sounded nervous as he spoke. "The Bile will make it so that he'll have to obey, even though he's one of Briggan's own, one of the Great Pack?"

"That's the whole *point* of this," the woman said exasperatedly. "If we wanted just any wolf for your spirit animal, there are plenty we could have used. Why do you think we're still here? Briggan's Silver Wolf talisman is with the army, already halfway back to the Reptile King by now, and yet we stayed behind."

"It wasn't so that you could back out now, I'll tell ya that," the man with the bat muttered, in the same peevish voice that Katalin remembered.

"Hush, Ugron," the woman hissed. She crouched down, beckoning the fox toward her, and it trotted over immediately. So it was hers, Katalin realized. There was something eerie about the way it obeyed her. Something very different from the loyalty that Tero showed her.

The woman spoke coldly. "Wolves can't normally be summoned as spirit animals, so putting one of Briggan's own into the thrall of a so-called *Conqueror* will send a strong message to him. When the 'Packleader' can't even control his own pack, he'll think twice before coming after his missing talisman, like Uraza and Jhi did."

"It'll be a message to *all* the Great Beasts, that they better not mess with us!" Mako exclaimed.

"Yes, that's what I said," the woman answered disdainfully. She extended a long arm that was covered in scars.

Even from her remove, Katalin could see the raised pink marks all over the woman's skin. She'd clearly been in more than her fair share of fights. With a brief flash of light, the fox leaped up, becoming a red ring around the woman's upper arm.

Katalin's mind was racing. The Reptile King was the man that she and the rest of their Marked resistance called the Devourer. He was the leader of the Conquerors, the one who had led his army through Zhong, through Nilo, and up into the edges of Eura. He was the one who gave the order to have her village sacked and burned.

And the curious thing about the Devourer's army was that all of them had spirit animals. No one Katalin had spoken to knew how this was possible. Their resistance was a small and scattered group *because* so few people ever summoned a spirit animal, and not all of those could be convinced to rise up against the Conquerors. So how had the Reptile King, from the relatively small continent of Stetriol, called forth a whole massive army of the Marked? Did the Bile have something to do with this? Katalin looked with renewed attention at the group huddled around the wolf.

"Now, are you ready to do this?"

"Yes," the young man said immediately. Then he hesitated. "Does it hurt?"

"You're a soldier," Ugron said. He spat on the ground. "Or at least, you've been passing for one."

"The taste makes our army rations seem like a treat," the woman said. "But I wouldn't peg you for someone with a discerning palate. Drink up!" She pulled a bottle out of a pouch at her waist and handed it to Mako. He held it up to the sky. In the light, the liquid looked murky and almost oily. Thick currents moved slowly through it.

Katalin couldn't let this happen. She touched the knife that she kept on her belt. It was sharp and could be deadly, but she knew she, Tero, and a knife were no match for three armed soldiers and two spirit animals.

Mako uncorked the bottle and sniffed gingerly at the liquid inside.

"This really smells bad," he complained, pushing the cork back in. "It smells like old garbage" – he wrinkled his brow, thinking hard, and then continued – "mixed with older garbage."

Katalin exchanged looks with Tero. He was ready for action too. She could feel his eagerness. They didn't have time to waste on coming up with a plan. Any second now, Mako would gather his courage and drink the Bile – and Katalin didn't want to see what would happen after that.

She placed her hand on Tero's back. With his velvety coat under her fingertips, she could feel the electric energy that zipped through him. Her anger at the treatment of the wolf focused into a thin line of energy that felt almost like joy. It was like a spear of fire that burned out any fear and doubt, and cracked her heart open into a feeling that was exhilaration and speed all at once.

That was when she realized they were moving, dashing side by side toward the clearing.

Tero headed straight toward Mako. With her senses clear and keen, Katalin could make a split-second decision about her own plan of attack, while noticing that the little mink was leaping, claws outstretched, at the bottle Mako held in his hands. Just as Tero made contact with the bottle of Bile, sending it flying out of Mako's hands and spinning away onto the ground, Katalin went into a slide aimed right at the legs of the scarred woman. Katalin took her right off her feet, and the woman came toppling down with a hard thud. Luckily, her fox was still in the passive state for the moment, and she was flustered enough not to be able to call him up right away.

Katalin froze for a moment, hand on her knife — it was wartime, but she had never harmed a human before. To her great relief, the woman was ignoring her, scrambling toward the bottle of Bile that was rolling away. With Mako, Tero, and the woman all lunging toward the bottle, Katalin took her chance. She dodged the large man as he came at her, using her speed and nimbleness to somersault right under him and toward the wolf.

It was yipping furiously now. Katalin was afraid to draw too close to it — its understandable rage at humans might well spill over to her right now — but she had to take the risk. She whipped her knife out and started sawing at the rope that bound its feet together. Her knife was sharp, but the rope was thick.

With a flash of perception, she could sense Ugron's hulking shape charging at her from behind, and spun around into a low crouch, her knife aimed up at him. He had his club in his hand, and it was poised to swing at her. Her knife would be useless. Katalin was sure it was all over for her. Then she became aware of a flurry of movement above her — the stupid bat!

Tapping into Tero's hunting instincts, she snatched the bat out of the air and clutched it to her chest, the knife tip pressed up against its tiny body.

"Stop right there," Katalin said, her voice somehow steady despite the potent rush of fear and excitement that filled her veins.

The man froze, his club in midair.

"Put down the club. If you even begin to swing that at me, I will slice your bat right open."

"Come on, little girl, let him go. You're outnumbered. You don't want to mess with us. Give up, and we'll have mercy on you and your skunk."

Katalin pressed her knife harder into the bat. It let out a pitiful squeak. She could feel its heart thudding against her palm.

"Okay, okay!" The man slowly put his club down on the ground and nudged it away with his toe.

"Farther!" Katalin grunted.

He kicked it away.

Katalin circled around the wolf so that she could keep the man in her sights, and attempted to go back to sawing through the rope while keeping the bat pinned against her. But the second her knife was off its body and on the rope, the bat started squirming and biting at her hand.

Out of the corner of her eye she could see Ugron hovering, torn between attacking her and playing it safe. Behind him, Tero was ducking and diving, a blur of movement. He was dodging the woman, her now-active fox, and Mako, and playing the ultimate game of keep-away with the Bile.

The wolf craned its neck back at her, snapping its jaws. Katalin gave the rope one last slash, and the constraints fell away. The wolf leaped up—for a split second Katalin was sure it was going to attack her—but then it simply shook out its fur, like a wet dog. It gave Katalin a gentle snarl and bounded away into the woods without a second look.

Her mission accomplished, Katalin lost her euphoric rush. She realized with a sinking feeling that she'd gotten herself into a terrible situation. They were outnumbered, and these Conquerors likely now knew she was a member of the Marked resistance. She was doomed.

As though he could read the realization in her face, Ugron took that moment to hurl himself at her, knocking her knife from her hand, then slamming her to the ground. She felt her back hit the earth with a sickening crack, and fingers of pain wrapped themselves around her. She looked frantically for Tero, craning her neck around Ugron's heavy bulk.

Now that the wolf was gone, Tero had stopped trying to keep the Bile out of the Conquerors' grasp, but he was in grave trouble himself. The mink was halfway up a tree, but the Conqueror's fox had Tero's tail between its teeth, and was shaking him down.

While he struggled, the woman approached with a burlap sack and scooped it over Tero, capturing him inside and tying it up with a tight knot.

"Well, that was a surprise," she said. Katalin could hear that she was trying to play it cool, but she was nearly breathless after the chase. "See what happens when you muck around, letting your fear hold you back, Mako? Things get messy."

Mako picked up the bottle of Bile and swung it back and forth. "Yeah, okay, I see. I'll drink it now."

"No, you fool," she snapped at him. "Now? There's no wolf now. You want to bond with a squirrel?"

"Calm down," Ugron said. "It'll be easy enough to capture another one of those mangy overgrown dogs. First we dispose of this green-cloak girl and her pet rat. Then we capture another one of Briggan's wolves and get this thing over with. We're not going back to the Reptile King until we've finished this."

He reached for the ropes that had bound the wolf, and easily tied Katalin's hands behind her back so that she could barely move.

"I'll do it," the woman said. She stalked over to a scabbard at the edge of the clearing and pulled out a long, gleaming sword. Katalin squirmed, but she couldn't free her hands. She tried to tap into her bond with Tero. More than ever before, she needed some of his clever thinking, his impulsiveness. She needed courage.

But she could feel nothing from him except for a mounting claustrophobia. Across the clearing, she could see his thrashing as he squirmed his small body against the sack.

"Head up, girl," the woman said, approaching with the sword. "Make it easier on yourself."

A prickling feeling raced up Katalin's spine. She thought it was fear, but then the now-familiar sound followed – the distant howling of a wolf. The proud, somber noise seemed to summon up some final bit of nerve in Katalin. She lifted her chin defiantly. She had saved one of Briggan's own wolves from these horrible Conquerors, and if she had to lose her life to them, well, she would show them the bravery of the resistance.

But then there was another answering howl, this one closer.

And another.

Suddenly the hill was echoing with howls, so that the sound became endless and swirling.

A pack of wolves burst into the clearing – maybe fifty or sixty, perhaps even a hundred. Katalin thought she saw coyotes and jackals and foxes too; she couldn't keep track of them all, though her eye was immediately drawn to the animal at the front. There was the wolf she had freed. She could recognize the white patches circling its eyes, and the look it gave her. It was not thanks, exactly, but the look of a proud creature repaying a debt.

Katalin stumbled back as the wolves tore at the Conquerors, a blur of gray and white fur. She felt a tug, and turned. One of the smaller wolves had the rope in its teeth and was yanking it off her hands. With a painful burn, the rough rope slid free. "Thank you," she gasped, already running away toward the sack that held Tero.

The wolf pack had so surrounded the three Conquerors that Katalin could barely see them through the flash of fangs and fur. She looked away, unable to stomach the scene, and unknotted the bag. She pulled Tero out gently. He immediately leaped onto his familiar place on her shoulder. She ran her hands over his body, checking for wounds, and sprinted toward the trees.

There, as massive and unmoving as a granite wall, was a huge wolf. He stood nearly as high as a house, and was looking down at her with eyes the color of sapphires.

Briggan.

"Normally," he said, in a voice that rumbled like a rock rolling down a hill, "normally, I would not allow a person to get this close to me."

For once, Tero was holding completely still. He was plastered low on her shoulder and staring up at the Great Beast in awe.

"Normally," Briggan continued, "I would flatten you with visions, make it so that you were unable to see the road in front of you for the dreams that would wrap themselves around your eyes.

"Normally, I would have my pack chase you from these hills before you had taken another step. Or I would have sent a landslide rumbling down, crushing your camp, so that you would have to retreat.

"But you put your own life on the line for one of my pack. I heard what you did, that you rescued him from a destiny worse than death, from a terrible bondage. And that you did so with no thought of repayment."

Katalin gave a tiny nod. She remembered Adelle's words, that she had to maintain her own courage and strength in the face of Briggan's enormous presence, so she spoke up. "Yes . . . sir. I did. With Tero's help." She inclined her chin toward the unusually meek mink.

"So then tell me," Briggan said, lowering his massive head down to her level. "What are you doing here? Why have you come all the way through the forest, across my valley, and into the Granite Hills, where no humans live?"

"I've come because we need you. Conquerors, people like the three who were trying to harm one of your pack, have come from Stetriol under the leadership of a terrible man called the Devourer. They have conquered Zhong, conquered Nilo . . . and soon they will conquer Eura, if you don't help us.

"I belong to a resistance of Marked people. Nearly all of us have bonded with a spirit animal. We wear green cloaks to distinguish ourselves from the enemy. But our forces are spread out, unorganized, and afraid. We need you to inspire and unite us. . . ."

As Katalin continued with her explanation of all the troubles in the world, she tried to read the expression in Briggan's great eyes. But he stayed as still and unreadable as a statue. Eventually she came to the end of her story. She had told him everything she knew of the Conquerors' activities, all the information that Adelle had coached her to say clearly and powerfully.

Briggan lowered his lids and bared his fangs in a terrible angry grimace.

It took all the courage Katalin had to stay standing in front of him when she wanted to turn and run. As she summoned it up, she could feel it—it was her own courage she was pulling on, not just Tero's—her own pride and defiance, her own burning wish for justice. In the face of the Great Wolf's sharp smile, each tooth like a spear, she stood tall.

"Thank you for seeking me out, Marked one," he said, his voice a low rumble. "These . . . *Conquerors* were not the first. Many of them passed through here recently. They stole something precious to me and escaped with it before I could hunt them all down. Only these three were foolish enough to stay. But I have one more question for you."

"Anything," Katalin said.

"Why you? Why are you here? Do you care so much about the fate of the world? Of politics, and Great Beasts, and wars that play themselves out on distant stages?"

She shook her head. "Briggan . . . Briggan, sir," she stuttered. "There is nothing distant about it."

"Tell me, what kinds of things have you seen in your mind since coming to my lands?" he asked her in a voice more gentle than any that she'd yet heard.

"My dreams are haunted by the same memories as always," Katalin answered. "I see my village burn again and again. I see my family . . ." She couldn't bring herself to say any more.

"You know, don't you, that I bring visions? I can help people catch a glimpse of their path. Of a *possible* path, of course. We always have the power to make change. I trust that you have seen clearly. If we allow the Conquerors to continue, there will only be more of what you've seen – more war. More burning."

She inhaled sharply. *"We?"*

"We," he said, his hackles rising. "I will help your Marked resistance in your ragged cloaks. I will form them into an army. The Greencloaks."

Briggan arched his neck back and let out a howl, a sound as big and powerful as the ocean. All around the mountain, echoing howls answered back – Briggan's pack, responding to his call.

Essix

FALL OF THE FOUR

By Brandon Mull

SOARING THROUGH A CLEAR BLUE SKY, ESSIX USED THE AIR currents to her advantage. The wind slid across her great feathers as she banked through an updraft to gain altitude in search of a stronger tailwind. Ahead, a forest spread out before her, a sea of green textures. Behind her raged the fiercest battle ever to stain the fields of Erdas.

The corpses of men and animals were piling up. Before the day was through, the tally would reach into the hundreds of thousands. In her mind, Essix could still see bodies torn by tooth and claw, pierced by shaft and blade.

She, Briggan, Uraza, and Jhi were all needed at the battlefront. Led by the Greencloaks, the four embattled nations of Erdas had united in a desperate offensive against the Conquerors. If the gamble worked, the Devourer would fall, along with Kovo and Gerathon. If not, the ever-growing army of Conquerors would sweep across the continents of Erdas, bringing the entire world under one domineering rule.

The three earthbound Great Beasts needed more time to reach the meeting place, so after they departed, Essix had lingered as long as she could, tearing into the Conquerors with her talons and helping the Greencloak armies adjust as the enemy commanders repositioned their forces. The warriors who had followed her to Stetriol, man and beast, needed her there for courage, for guidance, for protection. The Greencloaks would never have mustered the support necessary to mount this attack without her, Briggan, Uraza, and Jhi.

Now, in their hour of greatest need, she was leaving these armies behind. The Greencloak generals understood the reasons, and had communicated to their soldiers that their patron beasts were not abandoning them. Still, Essix had sensed the despair that fell over the Greencloaks as the Great Beasts withdrew from the battlefield.

Essix had almost stayed. The others could make her arguments on her behalf. She had no love of gatherings. But the appeals would not carry the same weight as they would coming from her. Like it or not, Essix knew how to read her fellow guardians better than anyone, and that could provide a meaningful advantage when persuasion was required.

In this dire hour, Tellun had finally summoned a Grand Council. If all the Great Beasts would stand together against the madness of Kovo and Gerathon, the outcome of the battle would be much more certain. This meeting was too vital to miss.

Below her, in the distance, the clearing came into view. Much of Stetriol was desolate waste or jagged red mountains. Only Tellun could have created such an idyllic forest on so harsh a continent in such a brief time. Stately trees surrounded a flat meadow where tall grass rippled in the breeze. A shallow stream meandered across the clearing, its bed a treasure trove of polished pebbles. A few bulky boulders added character.

The other beasts were there—all except Kovo and Gerathon, who had predictably shunned the proceedings, and Mulop, who would participate from afar. The octopus preferred not to travel, which freed the others to gather in noncoastal locations.

Trimming her wings, Essix plunged toward the meadow, the exhilarating speed focusing her thoughts. Until now, as a whole, the Great Beasts had chosen neutrality in the worldwide war. They had not met in a Grand Council since the early days, when Kovo and Gerathon appeared less directly involved and the Devourer was just beginning to reveal his unquenchable lust for world domination. This would be the last chance to gain meaningful assistance against the Conquerors. It would be no small task to steer this headstrong group toward war.

Essix alighted on a fallen log an instant before the sun reached its zenith—the appointed starting time. Her claws gripped the decaying wood much as a lesser falcon would cling to a branch.

"Cutting it close, are we not?" Cabaro remarked, stretching his golden form and extending his claws. As a physical specimen, none of the Great Beasts could quite match the lion. If he were not so arrogant and disinterested, he might have been their leader. None could rival him in battle. But he seldom roused himself to action, content instead to pursue a life of lordly leisure. Why hunt when he could feast on the spoils of the lionesses? Why fight when intimidation sufficed?

"I did not want to leave the battle," Essix said. "The free nations are hard-pressed. The fate of Erdas may well be determined before the sun sets."

"Does this mean we will be hurried?" said the enormous Dinesh, who looked more like a wrinkly gray hill than an elephant. "I did not cross the Deep to dash through a hasty conversation."

"The day you dash is the day I fly," laughed Suka. Sitting casually, huge paws in her lap, the polar bear looked to be in a playful mood. When she wasn't, all of Erdas needed to beware.

Essix resisted a laugh. Briggan, Rumfuss, and Uraza showed less restraint. Draped in silks, shaded by an embroidered canopy, the elephant looked like the exact opposite of haste.

"I came farther than anyone," Suka continued, "but a quick council suits me just fine."

"Fools mock," Dinesh said in a voice like the first tremors of an earthquake. "A Grand Council is no minor occasion. A certain dignity must be maintained."

A movement off to one side caught Essix's eye. She swiveled to see that a kangaroo had wandered into the clearing. All of the Great Beasts turned to regard the accidental visitor. The unfortunate kangaroo watched with paralyzed anxiety from the edge of the meadow. The poor creature knew it had made a fatal mistake. Essix could sense its heart rate accelerating.

The relative size of the kangaroo emphasized the enormity of the Great Beasts. Though fully grown and not a small specimen, the kangaroo would barely serve as a morsel for Cabaro. Only an excellent jump would allow it to brush against Tellun's belly. Next to the colossal bulk of Dinesh, the marsupial seemed no bigger than a chipmunk.

Tellun raised his head high, the tips of his magnificent antlers overtopping even Dinesh. "Let us begin," the elk announced. The Great Beasts lost interest in the kangaroo and came to attention. A hush fell upon all of nature. Even the nearby brook seemed to run quieter. Essix looked up at their leader, trying not to succumb to a sense of awe. Of all the Great Beasts, Tellun was the hardest to read.

"Not all . . . have come," Rumfuss complained.

"This is the appointed time and place," Tellun stated. "All were invited. Mulop declined to attend in person. Kovo and Gerathon gave no reply."

From the corner of her eye, Essix saw the kangaroo scamper away, taking advantage of the small mercy. Hopefully the animal would learn greater care from the experience.

"They're busy taking over the world," Briggan growled. "The battle is raging. Why are we here trading words while the fate of Erdas teeters?"

"The Great Beasts have never battled one another," Arax said firmly. The massive curls of his horns shone brilliant in the sunlight. "Let humans settle their own disputes."

Briggan began to pace. "Thanks to the Bile, this is not merely a human matter. The Conquerors have stolen animals from each of our spheres and brought them into bondage. Kovo and Gerathon openly aid the enemy in his bid for universal conquest. This war involves all life on Erdas."

Essix felt sorry for the wolf. Nearly the size of Cabaro, and close to his equal in combat, Briggan was a fighter, not a talker. He wanted nothing more than to rejoin the fray with his wolf pack. The tension was evident in his voice, his movements, his posture.

"Have we anything new to discuss?" Halawir asked. The eagle spoke in clear tones that commanded respect. Only Tellun had a more regal aspect. "When we last met, the Devourer was marshaling his forces with the backing of Kovo and Gerathon. The Bile was spreading. As a group, we elected to wait and see if humanity could quell the threat."

"Much has occurred since then," Uraza said, her voice quiet but intense. She held very still, but it was the stillness of a bowstring about to be released, the stillness of a predator before the pounce. "Many of our talismans were stolen. The Evertree was damaged. The spiritual link between man and beast has been put at risk. New bonds are forming, but they are twisted and painful. Young humans and the animals they bond with are becoming sick and deranged. Sometimes they die outright."

"You want to blame Kovo and Gerathon for damaging the Evertree?" Halawir asked. "Where is your proof? Such speculation is irresponsible. It sounds to me like the actions of conspiring men. How might men have gained access to your talismans? Perhaps because, against our counsel, the four of you have strayed too close to the humans."

"Too much familiarity with humans can be perilous," Suka warned. "We keep our distance for good reason."

"We're not the only ones who lost our talismans," Briggan reminded the group. "Where is yours, Halawir?"

The eagle spread his colossal wings in anger, and it was as if the sun had been swallowed by a storm cloud. The council fell into shadow – and silence – until Halawir regained his composure, tucking his wings back into place. "As could be predicted," the eagle replied, "once you awakened a desire for our talismans, the insatiable humans only craved more. Mine was stolen while I slept, taken from my very aerie. They are sly, these humans, that much is certain."

"Let humans . . . fight humans," Rumfuss said gruffly. The boar looked disgruntled. Essix had seldom seen him cheerful.

"This war involves more than humans fighting humans," Jhi said in velvety tones. "Kovo and Gerathon openly back the Devourer."

"The outcome will be determined today," Briggan said. "If the Greencloaks fall, the Devourer will take over the world. It was already too late to test our full strength against theirs. We mustered our best troops and bypassed the majority of the Conqueror armies to bring the fight to their homeland. The gambit is all or nothing."

"Why not wait to see if the assault works?" Dinesh asked.

"Because without our help, the Greencloaks will fall," Briggan snarled. "And without their help, we can't stop the Devourer."

"Nonsense," Arax protested. "If we decided to eliminate them, the thirteen of us could wipe out the ape, the serpent, and their human pet at our leisure."

"You do not appreciate their numbers," Jhi said calmly. "Their armies are fanatically devoted. Thanks to the Bile, every human soldier has a spirit animal bound to comply with any order. We are indeed powerful, but as a whole their might is greater. Envision a vast colony of ants bringing down an ox. This would be our fate."

"If we act now, we can end this threat," Essix said. "We'll never have to test whether we can defeat the Devourer on our own."

"And yet I remain unmoved," Cabaro said flatly. "The same four who urged for war in the last meeting are repeating themselves. Your involvement in human affairs has led to a devastating battle that you will probably lose. Now you want us to rescue you. You wish for your folly to overrule our prudence."

The council was quiet after this. Essix brought her sharp eyes to meet Cabaro's own, and despite his callous words, the lion was the first to drop his gaze. Something else was at work behind his protest, though she couldn't make out what.

"One Great Beast should not attack another," Dinesh declared. "Such a fight is unthinkable. It has no precedent."

Muscles bunching, tail swaying, Uraza responded in a poisonous tone. "You want to discuss breaking precedent? Great Beasts have never let humans decorate them with silks. Nor have they helped design shrines to themselves. Dinesh, I'm more interested in the opinions of Great Beasts who can find their own food."

Rumfuss exploded into laughter.

Dinesh raised his trunk indignantly. "I did not traverse the Deep to listen to—"

"You were shipped and dragged here by humans like cargo," Uraza spat. "You'd have handlers waving palm fronds at you right now if they weren't forbidden from Grand Councils."

Dinesh strained to his full height, long ivory tusks protruding like massive spears. The day dimmed. His voice was thunder. "Insolence! Defamation! Take that back this instant, or I, or I—"

"Will waddle out from under your canopy into the sunlight?" Uraza finished.

Tossing his huge head, Dinesh heaved his canopy to the ground. He trumpeted and the meadow quaked. Essix felt her feathers vibrating. "If you were worth the trouble, I'd trample you flat as a carpet."

"Would that not be one Great Beast opposing another?" Uraza replied smugly.

Rumfuss laughed gustily. "Got . . . you there!" he exclaimed. Few things amused the boar as much as arguments.

Dinesh sulkily plopped down on the grass. "A disagreement is not a war. Our views may differ. At times we get irritated and make idle threats. But we have never let our arguments escalate to violence."

Essix appreciated the point Uraza had made, but disagreed with the delivery. Dinesh was no closer to siding with them. If anything, the elephant was now further alienated. None of the Great Beasts lacked pride. Angering the others would not produce the desired result.

"The thought of Great Beasts fighting each other is abhorrent," Essix said. "We may not always agree, but we have always shared a mutual respect."

"Some more than others," Dinesh scolded, his wounded eyes on Uraza.

"We attend Grand Councils out of that same respect," Essix continued. "We cross great distances to confer together. But two of our number lacked the decency to attend today, though they were much closer to the meeting place than most of you."

"I miss Kovo," Suka said. "He told the best jokes."

"Their absence is hardly reason for war," Cabaro murmured.

"We established that this is the first time Great Beasts have opposed one another in battle," Essix said. She looked slowly around the circle, meeting the gaze of each of her fellows in turn. "But Great Beasts have also never caused such harm in the world. Our calling has ever been to protect and preserve Erdas, to seek balance, to limit tragedy—not to plunge the world into chaos. When have any of you stripped animals of their free will? When have you supported a tyrannical conqueror? Have you ever shamelessly ignored the warnings of Tellun and the other members of this council? Kovo and Gerathon have committed evils that are unthinkable to the rest of us. They remain unrepentant. Perhaps we must resort to unthinkable means to stop them."

Her eyes fell last on Arax the Ram, who stamped his

hoof. "All Great Beasts are free to act as we deem necessary," he said ardently. "No one of us is the lone guardian of Erdas. Not even Tellun. We each share a portion of that responsibility, and we each have our own methods and priorities. We counsel one another when necessary, but we do not compel. Kovo and Gerathon have made no move against any of us."

"Not directly," Jhi said. "But they have created war in our domains. And they have used the Bile to force animals in our care into servitude."

"We've all caused conflicts of one kind or another," Suka said. "Let the humans fight it out. This war could be just what we need. There are too many humans. They multiply on every continent, in every climate. They're drastically changing the balance. Their herds must be reduced. They take up too much space and consume too many resources. Humans are fast becoming the greatest plague Erdas has faced. Thanks to this war, humans are falling in greater numbers than we have ever seen. Perhaps we should celebrate."

"Humans are not our enemies," Tellun said, his voice effortlessly carrying more authority than any of the others could muster at their best. "They are fellow tenants of this world. Nature is full of hard realities. Predators and prey. Seasons of want and seasons of plenty. Humans have the right to survive and prosper as best they can. They have the same claim to Erdas as all creatures."

"Humans claim . . . too much," Rumfuss grumbled. "It will get worse."

"Our world is changing too quickly," Suka said. "There are many parts of Erdas I no longer recognize—beloved wilds where bears once roamed that are no longer open to us. Humans are the agents behind it. Perhaps Kovo recognizes the need to curb them."

"Different species rise and fall," Jhi said, her voice a soothing balm. Essix realized that if anyone could reach Suka through the walls of her quips and anxieties, it would be Jhi. The Great Panda was tranquility itself. "Some become dominant. Others go extinct. Humans *could* threaten the natural balance. They could also help preserve it. Although humans have great capacity for evil, of all species, they also possess the most potential for good. They are the most adept at putting the resources of Erdas to inventive use. Their ingenuity may cause problems, but it can also be a source of hope."

"Humankind will not overthrow the balance," Briggan said stoutly. "Not while we stand watch."

"But must we fight their battles for them?" Cabaro asked. "I'm with Suka – the more dead humans the better."

"Humans aren't all bad," Dinesh protested.

Suka chuckled. "Not when they worship you."

Dinesh bristled. "They don't worship me."

Suka laughed harder. "What about the temples, and the rituals, and the feasts in your honor? Don't worry, Dinesh. I love that you domesticate them!"

"I have long sought ways to work *with* humans rather than against them," Dinesh explained. "My methods have yielded some favorable results. Perhaps I have overplayed the role of enlightened mentor. I'll consider scaling it back."

"Humans," Rumfuss grunted. "Who can trust them?"

"I've found certain humans to be wonderful," Cabaro said slyly. "They're an acquired taste."

"Enough!" Briggan barked, sending eavesdropping birds scattering from the trees. "Right now, as we joke and argue, humans are fighting alongside animals to decide the fate of Erdas. Can we move the discussion forward?"

"A valid question has been raised," Essix said after an uncomfortable moment of quiet. "Should we celebrate when humans fall? It depends on which humans get removed. Some love Erdas as much as we do. Others seem determined to turn it into a wasteland. We must support the humans who have virtue and vision. Men and women like the Greencloaks, who partner with animals rather than rule them, who cherish the wild places as much as their strongholds. The Devourer represents the worst humanity has to offer. If he establishes himself as ruler of the five continents, all will suffer. We are the Great Beasts. It is our duty to protect Erdas, not to control it. Kovo and Gerathon have gone astray."

"Is this your argument?" Arax challenged. "We should move against the ape and the serpent because you feel they have gone astray? Where does such a judgment lead us? Who will be the next beast to offend the all-knowing falcon? Me? Dinesh? Cabaro? Perhaps Rumfuss. None of us love the boar. If popularity were vital, he would have been ousted long ago."

"Nobody . . . likes me?" Rumfuss exclaimed in surprise.

"You have few charms," Cabaro said silkily.

"Nonsense!" Rumfuss shouted. "I am . . . the best!"

"Cabaro sees little charm in anyone," Jhi said warmly. "Plenty of us like you just fine."

"Enlighten us," Cabaro dared her. "What is it you enjoy about Rumfuss?"

Jhi paused. Essix hoped she could find a compliment quickly. "Rumfuss is sturdy. He has little guile."

"The same could be said for a tree stump," Cabaro replied.

"Rumfuss is true to himself," Jhi continued. "He knows mercy. Beneath his rough exterior beats a good heart."

"I can bash . . . stone walls," Rumfuss grumbled. "I've . . . leveled forests. I eat . . . more than my weight. Spurn me. Be jealous. I care not. Envy . . . is the truest flattery."

"I'm with Arax," Halawir said. "What right have we to condemn one another? The last time we met in a Grand Council, the majority decision was to let the humans deal with the Devourer. Afterward, Briggan, Essix, Jhi, and Uraza disregarded that verdict and got involved. Should they not be condemned as well?"

"Go ahead and try," Uraza growled eagerly.

"You're far too ready to fight, Leopard," Dinesh admonished. "I grow weary of your warmongering."

"Do any of you believe that I love war?" Jhi asked.

The question silenced the group. Essix approved of the tactic. There had been too much speaking and not enough listening.

"I hate violence," Jhi said gently. "Even as a last resort, I find it revolting. So what would move me to join a battle?"

Nobody replied. Essix hoped Jhi had persuasive arguments ready.

"I detest something more than violence," Jhi continued. "Compulsion. Free will is our most fundamental right. Animals taken by the Bile lose their free will. They can't defend themselves. I know of no more terrible injustice.

I cannot allow such an imbalance to become universal. To do so would be to fail as a guardian of Erdas."

"None of us approve of the Bile," Ninani said.

All eyes went to the swan. She sat placidly upon the grass, as clean and pale as a lily. Essix had wondered when she might lend her voice to the proceedings. The falcon readjusted upon her perch, waiting for her to continue. Ninani seldom spoke. If Tellun inspired awe, Ninani evoked reverence. She was the kindest and gentlest of the Great Beasts, and by far the most graceful. Essix wished she would speak on their behalf, but the next few moments passed in silence. The swan said nothing more.

"Kovo and Gerathon are behind the Bile." Briggan finally spoke. "We asked them to dispose of it and they refused. Instead, they're using the Devourer to spread it across Erdas. We either stop the Conquerors today, or we watch as Erdas reaps the consequences."

"The way you paint the situation makes the choice seem clear," Cabaro said. "But how true are your colors? Don't Kovo and Gerathon deserve a chance to share their side?"

"This is their chance," Essix said. "They knowingly forfeited their opportunity to explain themselves. Instead they want to have their way by force. They are no longer protectors of Erdas. They are attempting to conquer it. And that makes stopping them our responsibility. We must tarry no longer. Let us hurry to the battlefront before the opportunity is lost!"

Tellun stirred, his antlers creaking like the bows of a great tree. The others waited for his pronouncement. "We have a grave decision before us," the elk said. "Do we unite against two of our own and halt the designs they have set in motion? Or do we trust that they remain guardians of Erdas with purposes outside our understanding?"

"I don't think I could kill Kovo," Suka said glumly. "I like him."

"You certainly could," Uraza growled. "As could Cabaro. As could Briggan. As could I. You may find him an acquired taste."

Essix cringed. It was the wrong moment for antagonistic humor.

Tellun snorted angrily. A charge filled the air, as if lightning might soon follow. "No matter our decision, I will not condone the slaying of a Great Beast. For one thing, it would be futile. While the Evertree stands, our destinies are tied to Erdas. If one form is lost, another will rise. If Kovo and Gerathon have betrayed their sacred duty, I would consider imprisonment, but not death."

"You four return to your battle if you wish," Dinesh said. "I'll not be joining you."

"Do you approve of the fight?" Briggan asked.

"I'm disengaging," the elephant said. "I will continue to protect my talisman. I will defend Erdas in my own way. The rest of you do as you will."

"How shocking," Uraza mocked. "At least have your worshippers pray for us."

"Let the humans . . . fight it out," Rumfuss grumbled.

"We mustn't move against Kovo and Gerathon unless they move against us," Arax said. "I felt that way before. I feel the same way now."

For a moment Essix had thought they might convince them. Even the most stubborn had wavered. Now she felt the opportunity slipping away, like a rabbit disappearing into its burrow. It was infuriating. The stakes were so high! The truth had been spoken plainly. They had made a strong case. But that did not compel the others to agree. "What about the innocent animals claimed by the Bile?" Essix asked.

"Are you new here?" Cabaro replied glibly. "What about the innocent bunny claimed by the fox? What of the blameless gazelle slain by the leopard? So some animals get forced into spirit bonds. That carries certain benefits. They're far from dead. We can't even every contest. Sometimes an animal can't fight back."

"I don't want to fight Great Beasts," Suka said. "Maybe if I was cornered. It just doesn't seem right to me."

"We should wait," Halawir said. "There is not enough evidence of wrongdoing from Kovo and Gerathon. It's too soon to condemn two of our own."

"I agree," Cabaro said. "I expect the four champions of humanity will fight on. But I shall not join them."

"That is six of the thirteen against," Briggan said. "Not yet a majority."

"Eight of fifteen if you count Kovo and Gerathon," Halawir said, his great yellow eye lingering on Cabaro a moment before moving to the wolf.

"They spurned this council and lost their say," Briggan insisted.

"The same tiresome four have spoken for war," Cabaro said. "Who else sides with the six?"

"Mulop has heeded our words from afar," Tellun announced. "He is content to let the four continue their campaign, and has no objection to the others abstaining."

"Seven of thirteen," Cabaro said.

"Tellun," Briggan implored. "Surely you will aid us. Surely you see the need. I have glimpsed the outcome of this day in a vision. If only the four of us stand against the Devourer, I fear it will end in darkness."

Rumfuss laughed brashly. "All days . . . end in darkness."

"I side with the majority of the council," Tellun said. "But I approve of you four continuing as you commenced. I know you sincerely mean to protect Erdas, just as I suspect Kovo and Gerathon do not. I will watch the battle closely. Should they cause you to fall, it will not be in vain."

"Will it take our deaths to convince you?" Uraza growled, rising lightly to her feet. Essix could feel her impatience finally coming untethered. The leopard had given up hope.

"It would be a start," Cabaro replied dryly. "My hunting grounds will nearly double."

Uraza surveyed Jhi, Essix, and Briggan, her violet eyes bright with anger. "We don't have to do this. We should let these fools inherit the world they deserve."

"Almost tempting," Briggan said.

"We can only control ourselves," Essix said. "We nudge others toward wisdom as best we can, but their decisions are theirs to make. It's often disappointing to try to influence others."

"That's the game Kovo and Gerathon are playing," Jhi said. "Asserting control over others. Over everything, perhaps."

"Shall we disappoint them?" Essix asked.

Briggan raised his head high. His deep blue eyes gazed at something that the rest of them couldn't see. Essix remembered the wolf's warning: This day would end in darkness. "I'll go alone if I must. While I live, Erdas has a protector."

"Not alone," Essix said, stretching her wings. "I won't abandon the people trying to stand against this evil."

"Nor will I," Jhi said. Her silver eyes were heavy for once, with some inner burden. "Though Suka might be of more use today."

"The four of us, then," Uraza said. "We've lost enough time."

Uraza launched herself away from the group, her sleek body elongating with every bounding stride. Without a backward glance, Briggan followed close behind. Jhi trundled after them at less than half their speed.

The wolf let out a resounding howl. Essix felt her heart fill with fire. The call echoed across Stetriol. Several of the Great Beasts hung their heads. It was hard to hear that battle cry without responding.

"Different day, same conversation," Cabaro remarked, stretching. He looked at Essix. "Not in a hurry?"

"I'll rejoin the fight well ahead of them," Essix said coolly. "I'm disappointed in all of you. If we can't unify against a threat this obvious, what purpose do we serve? Now that the matter is settled, let me share some final words. Mulop, you see more than you understand. Cabaro, you are a devastating waste of potential. I once mistook your pelt for golden, but it's clearly yellow."

The lion snarled, but did not even rise from his reclined position.

"Halawir," Essix continued. "You have all the manners of royalty, and none of the substance. I thought you, of all of us, would see the cunning work of Kovo behind the theft of our talismans. Something unforgivable has happened to us, cloaked behind the humans.

"Suka, hiding from tough choices is a choice; and, Rumfuss, never changing means never improving. Arax, how can you demand freedom for yourself but not for those in your care? Dinesh, don't let your greatness be only a matter of size.

"Tellun . . ." Essix paused, momentarily unsure how to proceed. The elk seemed unimpeachable. And yet . . . "I respect you, but I do not understand you. I fear you are too distant."

"And Ninani?" Cabaro asked expectantly.

Essix gazed upon the swan. "I believe that Ninani does her best."

"Fight bravely," Ninani said, her voice music for the soul. "If I had it in me, I would join you. For what it's worth, I believe you. I will help as I can."

Bolstered by the soft-spoken encouragement and disgusted by the others, the falcon spread her wings and took flight. As she gained altitude, the last remnant of conversation she caught was Dinesh inquiring whether it was time to eat.

Higher and higher she wheeled, seeking currents that would bear her more swiftly. The same sky that had hastened her journey to the meeting conspired to slow her return. At the limits of sight, the battle raged on, an ocean of carnage simplified by the distance.

The Grand Council had been a waste of effort. Of course she, Briggan, Uraza, and Jhi were returning alone. When action was required, brave individuals were infinitely preferable to committees. Essix scolded herself for believing the others could be swayed. Wishful thinking had clouded her judgment. They had lost valuable time.

Below her and somewhat ahead, Briggan and Uraza raced side by side. Jhi trailed behind, though closer than Essix had expected. The falcon grimly assessed the sky. Perhaps she had been overconfident thinking she would outpace the others back to the battle. Earlier in the day, the winds had seemed more neutral, with currents she could have used for her return trip. Now, high and low, far and wide, the air was against her.

Could one of the Great Beasts have manipulated the atmosphere? Neither Kovo nor Gerathon had that power, but Arax had some influence over the winds, as did Halawir. Essix cursed herself. She should have withheld her criticisms.

The winds were not enough to defeat her, but they were a nuisance. It made the return trip a grueling chore. If the unfavorable currents persisted, even Jhi might rejoin the battle ahead of her.

As she muscled her way forward, Essix watched wolves mass around Briggan, howling with joy at the return of their Packleader. Curiously, a human Greencloak girl ran along with the wolves, wearing an expression of mad exhilaration. Her black mink spirit animal dashed excitedly beside her. Even from high above, Essix could sense Briggan's resolve spreading through the pack. She had never felt such determination from the wolf. It almost made her feel sorry for the Conquerors.

The closer Essix came to the battleground, the clearer she saw how far the conflict had progressed. The

Greencloaks' forces had pressed forward in a valiant attempt to reach the Devourer. As a result, the enemy had given them ground, then closed in from the flanks, unleashing all of their reserves. Surrounded and losing momentum, the beleaguered Greencloaks were about to be annihilated.

Then Briggan reached the field, slamming into the enemy like an avalanche, backed by a horde of wolves. Uraza came with him, ravaging Conquerors everywhere she ran. The enemy army buckled, some fleeing, some turning to face the new threat. It bought time for the main body of the Greencloaks, allowing some of them to push nearer to the Devourer.

Corpses accumulated in drifts. Blood muddied the ground. Animals and humans clashed and fell.

Sacrificing altitude to knife forward against the headwind, Essix approached the front of the battle where Gerathon, Kovo, and the Devourer awaited their foes. A hulking mound of muscle, the ape clutched a huge club and shouted a challenge at the onrushing Greencloaks. Sinuous and menacing, Gerathon coiled and reared up, flaring her broad hood. Clad in foreboding armor, the Devourer drew his sword, his enormous saltwater crocodile at his side.

The Greencloak charge was losing momentum. The Devourer's bodyguards held them, and then began driving them back.

Far across the battlefield, Jhi raised up, paws swaying. The enemy defenders seemed to lose vigor. A bold cluster of Greencloaks surged forward, steel ringing against steel, claws raking, teeth biting.

Club held high, Kovo stalked forward to deal with the oncoming Greencloaks. Thanks to his size, a few swipes of his weapon would end the attack. Briggan got there first, an unstoppable fury of fangs and claws. The ape staggered back. Briggan's jaws found the arm with the club. The weapon fell and the ape cowered as Briggan stood over him, hackles raised, crimson teeth inches from his throat.

The wolf did no more. His mandate from Tellun was to capture, not to kill, so he stood over the ape, paws on his chest, holding him in check.

Then Essix saw him – a lean Niloan warrior, only lightly armored, but lithe and quick, nimbly dodging through the ferocious maze of combat. Carrying only a slender spear, the warrior refused to engage any combatant, deflecting blows and bodies with his weapon rather than attacking. Stepping lightly, moving surely, he weaved through the skirmish, a fragile twig somehow surviving a violent stretch of rapids. Essix recognized him as Tembo, the Niloan goat thief who had become the human leader of the Greencloaks. Her keen eyes could see that his vervet monkey spirit animal was resting as a tattoo upon his arm. So where had this uncanny agility come from?

Something about the way the Niloan moved drew Essix's gaze back to Jhi. Defended by Greencloaks, the panda remained in a meditative state, swaying rhythmically. Conquerors came at Jhi left and right, but she was well-guarded, especially fiercely by a Zhongese young woman with a pied starling on her shoulder. Improbably, the girl fought with her eyes closed, as if sensing her attackers by sound alone. In a flash of insight, Essix recognized the connection between the sprinting Niloan warrior and the panda. Jhi was with him, enhancing his natural gifts, heightening his senses. No wonder he flowed through the intense combat with such otherworldly grace!

Conquerors rushed to attack Briggan and free Kovo. The wolf had outdistanced his pack, losing his fellow canines as they became mired in the tumult of battle. As the first Conqueror blows fell, Uraza arrived, tearing into the attackers savagely.

Then Gerathon struck, entwining her long body around the leopard in a desperate squeeze. Struggling against the deadly embrace, Uraza became vulnerable not only to Gerathon's fangs, but to Conqueror spears and swords.

Essix had almost reached the skirmish. She dived recklessly downward, holding her silence to attack with surprise.

The Devourer flung his sword to Kovo. The blade skittered over the ground, coming to a halt just within the ape's reach. As Briggan turned to snap at a bothersome soldier, Kovo slashed the wolf's throat, following the murderous strike with further stabs and slashes.

Essix felt each blow as if it had torn her own flesh. The enraged ape lunged to aid Gerathon. Essix tried to hasten her approach, but the wind surged against her. Uraza thrashed against the serpent as Kovo plunged the sword again and again. With the ground rushing closer, Essix glanced back to see Jhi's Greencloak guardians crumbling. A host of weapons pierced the docile panda, who continued to hold her trancelike focus despite the injuries.

Tembo, the Niloan warrior, had almost reached the Devourer, spear poised to throw. But the saltwater crocodile darted forward, vicious jaws agape. Facing certain doom, the warrior lost his path to the enemy commander.

Essix landed on the crocodile like a whirlwind, her talons tearing at its long jaws.

Sidestepping the scuffle, Tembo came within range and hurled his spear. The sleek weapon found a gap in the armor, impaling the Devourer, who staggered and fell. In that moment King Feliandor looked to Essix like the boy he truly was – a young man caught up in schemes he barely understood. But boy or not, he was the human leader of the Conquerors. And now he was gone.

Essix could only rejoice for an instant.

Club now in hand, Kovo descended upon her. Despite her considerable size, the falcon's bones were relatively light and fragile. As Jhi fell in the distance, Essix's body shattered beneath the onslaught.

Left to die, time skipped along in disjointed intervals. Essix heard Kovo shouting in frustration as his soldiers broke ranks. Why were the Conquerors losing heart? Was it the fall of the Devourer?

Essix found it hard to breathe. The scavengers of Stetriol would be the big winners today. Tonight they would feast like kings!

High above, a speck circled, almost at the limit of Essix's sharp vision. Halawir? Was the eagle here? Was she imagining it?

And then the presence washed over her, like sunrise, and new life, and the cleansing calm that follows mourning. She did not need to see Tellun to know he had arrived. No wonder the Greencloaks had taken heart! No wonder the enemy quailed!

Kovo screamed in frustration. The cries were distant, muted, fading.

Essix could not open her eyes, but she felt the warm breath of the nostrils near her face. Was Tellun trying to heal her? She was too far gone, ruined inside. The elk should help the others. Then, reaching out with what remained of her senses, Essix discovered that Jhi, Briggan, and Uraza were already gone.

Essix failed once more to open her eyes. She was slipping away, but she heard Tellun speak.

"Rest for a season, noble falcon. You have served Erdas well. As you will serve her again."

And then there was quiet.

Essix rested in the tranquil stillness. She had no desire to rouse her mind. Time lost all meaning. The silence was peaceful and good.

And then, as if dawn had broken, there was a light. A great radiance exploded around her, shifting and liquid, noisy with the gasping of human voices.

Essix opened her eyes, startled by the brilliance, and in it she saw the lean, tan face of a boy, grimy but shrewd. His eyes watched hers with astonishment.

Interesting, Essix thought. With a flurry of wings, she leaped up to the boy's shoulder and gently pinched her claws into his skin.

BOOK SIX:

RISE AND FALL

Deep in a vast desert waits one of the most
powerful and dangerous of all the Great Beasts:
Cabaro the Lion. With the team shattered,
stealing the giant lion's talisman seems
impossible. But what choice do they have?

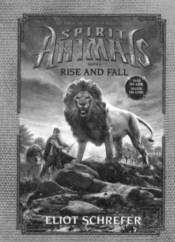

Each book unlocks in-game rewards.
Log in with your copy to help save Erdas!

The Legend Lives in You

You've read the book — now join the adventure at **Scholastic.com/SpiritAnimals**!

Enter the world of Erdas, where YOU are one of the rare few to summon a spirit animal.

Create your character.

Choose your spirit animal.

THE LEGEND LIVES IN YOU